"I want y'all to find a bunch of people to be praying for my dad... to find a girlfriend."

"Not on the church-wide prayer chain, Chelsea," Faith protested.

"His whole life is this town and me—specifically keeping me his overly safe little girl. I want him to have some fun."

Faith wasn't sure how she felt about it. Surely it was a good plan. But a girlfriend? On the prayer chain?

"What do you think, Faith?" Chelsea asked.

"When would he have time to go out?"

"That's the point. He needs to make time. To be *forced* to make time."

Faith wasn't so enthused. All she could think about as she waved goodbye to Chelsea was that Gabe would be angry. And she would be miserable.

But why would watching Gabe go out and have fun make her miserable? Did she feel more than a neighborly connection with Gabe? More than friendship?

Books by Missy Tippens

Love Inspired

Her Unlikely Family
His Forever Love
A Forever Christmas
A Family for Faith

MISSY TIPPENS

Born and raised in Kentucky, Missy met her very own hero when she headed off to grad school in Atlanta, Georgia. She promptly fell in love and hasn't left Georgia since. She and her pastor husband have been married twenty-plus years now, and have been blessed with three wonderful children and an assortment of pets. Nowadays, in addition to her writing, she teaches as an adjunct instructor at a local technical college.

Missy is thankful to God that she's been called to write stories of love and faith. After ten years of pursuing her dream of being published, she made her first sale of a full-length novel to the Steeple Hill Love Inspired line. She still pinches herself to see if it really happened!

Missy would love to hear from readers through her website, www.missytippens.com, or by email at missytippens@aol.com. For those with no internet access, you can reach her c/o Steeple Hill Books, 233 Broadway, Suite 1001, New York, NY 10279.

A Family for Faith

Missy Tippens

Love Inspired

Recycling programs for this product may not exist in your area.

ISBN-13: 978-0-373-81543-2

A FAMILY FOR FAITH

www.LoveInspiredBooks.com

Printed in U.S.A.

And now these three remain: faith, hope and love.
But the greatest of these is love.

—1 *Corinthians* 13:13

There is no fear in love, but full-grown love turns fear out of doors and expels every trace of terror! For fear brings with it the thought of punishment, and he who is afraid has not reached the full maturity of love.

—1 *John* 4:18

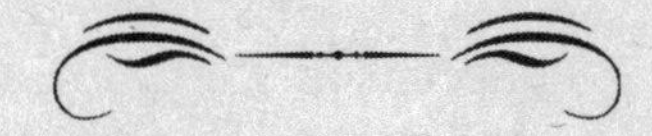

To my two wonderful sons—
both amazing young men. And to
my wonderful daughter—a joy at
age thirteen. Thank you for making life so fun!

To my husband for unwavering love and support.

To God for allowing me a career I love so much.

To the father and daughter on the flight from D.C.
to Atlanta who inspired this story.

Acknowledgments

Thanks to Lindi Peterson, Ruthy Logan Herne
and my sister-in-law for research assistance.

As always, I owe a huge debt of gratitude
to Emily Rodmell and the team at Love Inspired.

Chapter One

Gabe Reynolds paced the photo-lined hallway, back and forth past baby and childhood pictures of his daughter, past the door where that same daughter did whatever preteen girls did behind closed doors. Considering the amount of time he spent coaxing her out of there these days, he figured he'd wear a path in the finish of the hardwood floor by the time his only child was grown and gone—something he intended to delay as long as possible.

He finally stopped and banged on the bathroom door. "Hurry up, Chels. You'll be late."

His dear, sweet daughter growled at him. *Growled.*

With a badge on his chest and weapon at his hip, he *should* be prepared to deal with anything. But give him a drunk or a thief any day over this soon-to-be-teenage-girl business.

He pounded the door again. "I've gotta get back to the station. What are you doing in there?"

"For the thousandth time, I'm coming."

He knew without a doubt that she was in there rolling her eyes at him. "What's taking so long?"

"A work of art takes time," she said in her best theatrical voice. Then she giggled, more like her normal, little girl self.

This switching from girl to young woman then back to girl in the blink of an eye was making his head spin. "You better not be putting on makeup."

"I'm a teenager. All my friends wear makeup."

"You're not thirteen yet. And if all your friends jumped off—"

She yanked the door open so fast it banged into the wall. She glared at him. "No. If all my friends jumped off a bridge, I would *not* jump, too. This is totally different and you know it."

Her cheeks glowed with a too-bright pink that matched her tinted lips. Her mascaraed eyelashes, clumped into several uneven spikes, seemed a mile longer than usual. She looked grown-up. Too grown-up—the kind that would attract the attention of guys. "All I know is I forbade you to wear makeup and... and..." He jabbed his finger at the pile of containers on the bathroom counter. "That looks an awful lot like makeup. Where'd you get it?"

She huffed and tossed her dark curls over her shoulder. "I bought it with my allowance. And I'm learning to put it on so it *accentuates* my best features."

She was accentuated, all right. And sounded like

she was spouting something she'd seen on an infomercial. He squinted as he checked out her face, so much like her mother's it made it hard to look sometimes. And even though he had the urge to drop the subject and run the other direction, it was his job to deal with this kind of situation now. "You've got on lipstick. Wipe it off."

"I want to look nice for our youth group meeting at the church tonight."

"Why?"

She shrugged. "No reason." She fingered a small picture frame on the counter, then quickly placed it facedown before he could see whose photo it held. "Now, please let me finish. I'll be out in five minutes."

A boy. It had to be because of a boy. "Who is he?"

"Who's who?"

"The boy. The one you're putting makeup on for."

She rubbed a finger with brown sparkly goop over her eyelid. "No one. I'm doing it for myself."

"Hand it over."

She sighed and slapped a little compact into his hand. "There, are you happy? No more eye shadow."

"No. Hand over the photo. Of the boy." He reached toward the picture frame.

"No!" She stopped him by grabbing hold of his hand. She looked terrified.

Which terrified him. If the guy was some high school punk, Gabe would be out the door and into the squad car in five seconds flat.

He shook Chelsea's hand off and grabbed the gold frame. But he didn't find some guy. All the frustration and fear whooshed out of him along with his breath when he found his wife. His sweet, beautiful wife.

Once he recovered his equilibrium, he said, "Chels, why do you have your mom's picture in here?"

She gave a little shrug, this time not so rebellious. "I told you. I'm learning to put on makeup."

Pain steamrolled him flat to the floor as he remembered Chelsea watching her mom put on lipstick on Sunday mornings before church and often asking if she could have some. Tina would smile, kiss a pink lip print on Chelsea's cheek and promise to show her when she got older.

Now here their daughter was, studying Tina's face, learning to apply lipstick by herself. Gabe ached for Chels. Ached period.

It had been five years since the accident, and just when he was making headway and felt like he might finally be able to breathe again, this had to happen.

"Please, Dad?" She took the frame from his hand and held the photo up beside her face. "See? I tried to do just what she did."

He wanted to hug her. To protect her from any

more pain in her young life. She needed her mom, especially for moments like this. But no, all she had was a cop dad who didn't have a guess at how to handle his daughter growing up. He swallowed, then cleared his throat. "I'm sorry. But you're just not old enough. You'll have to wash that stuff off your face."

She heaved a sigh that seemed to start at her toenails. "Okay." She stared at the photo for a second. "Do I look pretty?" She'd said it so softly he wasn't sure he heard her right. But then she turned to him and waited, looking everywhere but directly at him.

Oh, boy. "Well, now, I guess you better let me get a good look at you."

She smiled shyly as she looked up, but then the smile went crooked as she gnawed on her lip. He had a feeling she wasn't quite as comfortable being in makeup as she thought she would be.

"You look beautiful. Always."

"I do look a little like Mom, don't I?"

He breathed in through his nose, then forced a smile. "Even prettier."

"Thanks." She threw her arms around his waist, and for a split second, all was as it should be. Or at least it was back to the norm of the last few years. It would never again be *as it should be.*

He gave her a quick pat on the back before stepping away.

A horn honked outside. Chelsea's ride to church.

"Hurry. You know Gary and Audra have other kids to pick up."

"Go tell 'em I've got to wash my face and to wait up."

"Okay. Hey, I'm making your favorite dinner this evening. Tomato soup and grilled cheese sandwiches."

She splashed water on her face. "Daaad. You know we eat at church. And I guess I forgot to tell you a bunch of us are hanging out tonight after the meeting."

All he could do was groan as he walked away. Why couldn't everything just stay simple? Go to work. Come home. Eat dinner. Watch a little TV. Go to bed. But Chelsea had insisted on staying involved in the church.

The youth counselors had been kind to offer to drive her every week. Of course, they volunteered for everything at the church while he, on the other hand, didn't even make it to Sunday-morning worship on the rare Sundays he was off.

The services didn't feel right with that empty seat beside him.

When he stepped outside, the hot, humid air slapped him in the face. Another stifling July evening in Corinthia, Georgia, that made him long for winter. A blue Ford sat in his driveway with the engine running. It looked like the one that belonged to his next-door neighbor, Faith Hagin.

She rolled down her window and waved. "I'm filling in for Audra and Gary tonight."

"She'll just be a minute," he hollered.

Faith had bought the local coffee shop and moved to town about a year ago. Though she tended to keep to herself, he'd gotten to know her a little as they worked in their yards and through his daily visits to her café for coffee and homemade pastries. They mainly talked about work, but he'd found out bits and pieces about her family.

He'd learned she was divorced and had a teenage son. For some reason—and Gabe hadn't pried—the boy lived with his dad. Gabe hadn't pushed Faith on the topic as they'd gradually formed a sort-of friendship. He figured it wasn't his business. But if she was going to be helping with the church youth…

Chelsea barreled outside. As she spotted the car, she came to a stop. "Is that Faith?"

"Yes. Looks like she's driving tonight."

"Cool." Chelsea went around to the passenger side of the car as Gabe ambled to Faith's open window. Air-conditioning blasted him in the face.

"I'll bring her home by nine," she said.

"Why so late?"

Chelsea rolled her eyes and shook her head, exasperated. "I told you. We're hanging out."

He wasn't positive, but it looked as if Chelsea had reapplied the pink lipstick. He squinted, trying to see better, while worrying about her "hanging out" with a group that included high school-age youth.

Ignoring the possible makeup infraction for the moment, he asked Faith, "Where are they hanging out?"

Faith gave him a sympathetic smile and he once again wondered about her relationship with her son. It seemed she understood his worry. "At the café tonight for some decaf and live music."

He'd heard her coffee shop was turning into a regular teen hangout. But Chelsea, too? "As long as you're there with them…"

"Of course." She pointed at the seat belt to remind Chelsea to buckle. "She'll be fine."

"Thanks." He leaned inside the window and couldn't help but notice how good it smelled inside. He filled his lungs and wondered if his daughter was wearing perfume. But he hadn't smelled it in the house.

He glanced at Faith and, for the first time, wondered if *she* wore makeup. He couldn't really tell for sure. She was a natural beauty, with light brown hair she pulled into a ponytail and gorgeous greenish-blue eyes. He'd never noticed her wearing that particular flowery fragrance.

She shifted the car into Reverse. "You know, if you're worried about her, I hear they're always looking for more volunteers to help with the youth."

Why did someone bring that up every single week? It was all he could manage to drop off Chelsea on Sunday mornings.

Time for a subject change. "New perfume?"

She seemed surprised, but then she raised her eyebrows as if impressed. "Ah, so you're a master of avoidance."

His sweet daughter snorted a laugh. "Yep. Avoiding me growing up."

He snapped his mouth closed on his automatic rebuttal and decided he wasn't going to get drawn into that trap. Though, surely Faith would see his view on the subject. "See you at nine." As he patted the car door to let them leave, Chels smiled at Faith, and a sheen of forbidden gloss on her pink lips flickered in the evening sun.

They honked and waved. As they drove away, toward the church, he realized just how empty his world was whenever Chelsea left. Eventually, he'd have to "get a life" as Chels always told him. But for now, he had to focus on her—and on figuring out how in the world she had managed to pull one over on him yet again.

Faith wasn't sure how the youth counselors, Gary and Audra, had roped her into driving the group of kids. She planned to help this once, then get back to service more in line with her gifts—cooking, cleaning, volunteering in the church office…

After picking up the last child who needed a ride to the Sunday-evening youth group meeting, Faith observed the four middle schoolers in her vehicle, the two girls giggling and the two boys jostling each other around. Her son, Ben, had moved in with his dad five years ago, during seventh grade. Watching the seventh and eighth graders interact made her ache for what she'd missed. Of course, Ben hadn't been in a good place in seventh grade. He'd hooked up with a bad crowd and hadn't taken part in the joyful laughter and harmless teasing this bunch of kids enjoyed.

Like the oppressive humid air, guilt settled over her, pressing her into the contours of the car seat, making it difficult to breathe…reminding her what a failure she'd been.

She forced air into her lungs and tried not to think of the past. Ben was doing great now and that's what mattered.

"We're here." Faith dropped the noisy middle school youth at the back of the church where they found the others outside throwing a fluorescent-green Frisbee. "I'll see you for coffee later."

"Thanks!" they called as they piled out of her SUV.

Her pastor, Phil, flagged her down as he pulled a cloth hanky out of his pocket and swiped it across his brow and into his graying temples. "As you may have heard, Audra and Gary are moving, so I could really use your help with the youth."

Teens dealing with peer pressure, sex, drugs. Dealing with crises of faith. Asking my advice…

It pained her to tell anyone *no* when they needed her. Especially Phil, who had been kind and tried to make her feel welcome from the day she moved to town. But as much as she loved kids and would like to help, there was no way she was prepared for a youth leadership position. If Phil knew her track record with Ben, he probably wouldn't even ask.

Besides, her work schedule wouldn't permit it. "Phil, you know I'd do anything—clean the church, produce the bulletin, cook the meals. But with my café to run I can't make such a big weekly commitment."

"Think about it. They'd really like you."

"I'm sure I'd love them. But this summer is crazy enough with getting ready for Ben's visit."

"Maybe in the fall." He waved goodbye as he headed toward the air-conditioned building. "Hey, I look forward to meeting Ben."

Yes, Ben. Her number one priority continued to be her relationship with her son. Soon to be a senior, he would graduate and move off to college before she knew it. Since he lived forty-five minutes away with his dad—and lived and breathed baseball year-round—time with him was scarce. He'd be coming soon to stay for two weeks. She couldn't wait, especially since he'd canceled his visit the previous summer. After having to settle for quick trips to ball games or his dad's house for the past year, she looked forward to uninterrupted time together and wanted it to be perfect.

First on her to-do list was to train Natalie to run

the café while Faith was on vacation with her son so she could give him undivided attention.

It was her last chance to heal their relationship.

"I need a life," Chelsea said later that night as Faith drove toward home, the last orange and pink rays of the sunset fading on the horizon.

Join the club, she almost said without thinking. Thirty-four years old, divorced half a lifetime ago from a man who chose the partying college life over his wife and new baby, with a nearly grown son who acted like she didn't exist. Yes, she also needed a life. "Give your dad a break. He's used to the little girl who depended on him for everything."

She sighed and looked at Faith with twinkling brown eyes—more like milk chocolate than the dark chocolate of her father's. "I had so much fun tonight. Why can't he let me hang out with my friends more often?"

"You're twelve, not sixteen. Be patient."

With arms crossed and head shaking, Chelsea *tsked,* sounding and looking like an adult. "Twelve is old enough to spend the night at my best friend's house. He won't even let me do that. And he caught me putting on makeup today and made me wash it off."

"You're beautiful without it." Just like her mother had been. Faith had seen the photos in Gabe's living room.

It had to be tough for a girl Chelsea's age to go

through so many life changes without a mom around. Though Faith's dad deserted them when she was about the same age, at least she'd had her mom during that transitional time.

"Well, I like wearing makeup. And it's going to be a constant battle. Unless..."

She cut a glance in Chelsea's direction. "Unless what?"

"Unless you help me."

Oh, boy. Even though she and Gabe had formed a bit of a friendship over coffee, he'd always been private where family matters were concerned. He would not want her butting in. "I'm sure he's doing what's best for you."

"I don't think he'd be so stubborn if my mom were here. So maybe if you could sweet-talk him about the makeup...and about letting me hang out at the café..." She turned and pretty much begged with her big brown eyes.

Faith shouldn't get involved. She had her own family mess to deal with and might cause a bigger one with Gabe's family.

But poor Chelsea. It did sound like Gabe was being overly protective. And she knew personally how that could backfire. He could certainly stand to give Chelsea a little bit of freedom. "If I get the chance, I'll see what I can do."

Chelsea squeezed Faith's arm and squealed. "Thank you!"

Of course, Faith had heard the stories of how

Chelsea nearly died in the auto accident that killed her mother. She'd spent months in the hospital and rehab. Faith would probably be protective, too, in that situation.

Just thinking about it brought back memories of worrying about her son when he moved two hours away from her former home in Augusta to live with his dad and stepmom in Atlanta. *Will they love him as much as I do? Will they discipline him like he needs? Will they protect him?*

What utter helplessness…and rejection. Pain she never wanted to feel again.

When she and Chelsea arrived at the house, Gabe stood on his front porch with his arms crossed in front of him. "You're late."

"I'm sorry." Faith's watch showed a mere ten minutes after nine. "Had to get the café ready for the morning."

"Understandable. But Chels, you should have called."

"I would've if I weren't the only person on earth without a cell phone." She smirked at him and, judging by his scowl, it was not a good thing to do at the moment.

"The café has a landline. Now go on in and get ready for bed."

"Man, I was just teasing." With all the earlier joy wiped off her face, she stomped inside and slung the door shut with a bang.

Let it go, Faith. Don't butt in.

But she'd promised Chelsea. "Gabe, may I offer a suggestion?"

She couldn't read his expression as he recrossed his arms. For a second, she thought he would refuse.

"I guess," he said instead.

He didn't exactly look receptive, but she plowed ahead anyway. "Lots of kids Chelsea's age are allowed to do things with their friends. Could you maybe consider giving her a little wiggle room?"

"If you give an inch..."

"She's a good girl."

"And she's also strong willed."

Faith knew a whole lot about strong-willed children. She'd tried to raise one and had struggled the whole time. "You can't be too hard on Chelsea or she might rebel."

Memories of Ben storming out of the house—and stumbling back in—brought a wave of nausea. Who was she, a total failure at motherhood, to give advice?

He stared into her eyes as if he was thinking it over. But then the staring went on just a moment too long and she felt like she was being examined. Could he see through to the real Faith Hagin?

She tightened her ponytail as the chirping of the cicadas crescendoed in the otherwise silent night. She shoved her hands into the back pockets of her jeans to keep from fidgeting. "What?"

"I'm just trying to figure out if you wear makeup."

Makeup? "I, uh, don't usually wear makeup. It's

too much trouble when I have to go to work so early. But I did put on a little for church this morning."

He stepped closer, gently took hold of her chin and tilted her face up so he could see better in the porch light. But his touch didn't linger and he acted surprised to have done it.

She backed up a step. "I could teach Chelsea how to apply basic cosmetics—enough to appease her." Faith's face blazed with heat, especially where he'd touched her.

His dark brown eyes bore into hers, as if he still held her under a microscope. A searing blush crept to her chest and seemed to squeeze her heart.

He finally blinked and stepped back toward the door. "You're a natural beauty. I don't see much difference between most days and Sunday."

His matter-of-fact declaration made her heart skip a beat or two.

Before she could put two coherent words together, he shook his head. "Thanks for the offer, but no. I'm not going to give on the makeup issue."

Scattered thoughts—*he thinks I'm a natural beauty?*—ricocheted around in her head. But she managed to refocus on Chelsea. "She's almost a teenager, Gabe. You'll have to start letting go eventually."

He straightened up into his big, bad Chief of Police stance. "She's my daughter. I know what's best for her."

And she'd thought she'd known what was best

for her son. She'd been very protective of him, too. Trying to make sure he didn't go down the drinking-and-partying path his dad had gone down many years before. But her controlling had pushed Ben in the opposite direction.

For some reason, she needed to make Gabe understand. "Yes, you do know what's best. But sometimes, knowing best doesn't matter. If we smother them and don't give them room to become independent, we set them up to make bad decisions."

He studied her through squinted eyes, this time with suspicion. "You sound like you speak from experience."

"Yeah. I'd been left by my dad and my husband and thought if I worked hard enough I could hang on to my son. But it pushed him right into a group of friends who were an awful influence."

She snapped her mouth shut before she revealed more. The townspeople knew Ben lived with his dad and that he was too busy with sports to come visit. But she'd never shared with anyone the details of her son's problems in middle school, about his begging to live with his dad in Atlanta—about how he thrived once he moved there. When she moved to Corinthia a year ago to be closer to Ben, it was also to get away from the years of strange looks from former friends, to get away from the sideways glances. *What's wrong with Faith that her son did so poorly in her care, then had a complete turnaround when he got away from her?*

"I'm sorry, Faith. I didn't realize all you've been through," he said. "I'll keep your advice in mind."

She'd promised Chelsea she'd try to talk to him and she had. Duty fulfilled. "Okay, then. Good night." She hurried down the porch stairs and along the front walk. By the time she reached the grass between their houses, she heard footsteps behind her.

"Hold up a second, Faith." When Gabe reached her, he shoved his hands into his pockets. "Look, I'm sorry. I appreciate your offer to help. I do. But…" He looked at his feet. At the sky. At her house. "I know you're right about Chelsea. In my head, I know it. But in here—" he thumped a fist on his chest "—I can't go there yet."

Her heart ached at the look of pain on his face. "Children can do that to the best of us."

"Yeah." He rocked back on his heels. "I guess I actually could use your help. Some female guidance for Chelsea since she's been pushing for independence. I've got to do something. I can't let her…" His voice hitched.

Why, Lord? Why get me involved in this? She wished she could simply tell him good luck and turn away. But as if God Himself were forcing the words out of her mouth, she said, "What can I do?"

The breath huffed out of him and his tense expression eased. He laughed. "I have no idea."

His smile ravaged her already tender nerves. She'd always thought he was handsome. Especially when in uniform. But seeing him in angst over his young daughter sent his attractiveness to a whole new level.

"Well, I can tell you she was glowing with happiness after hanging out at the café tonight. Anything you can do to let her spend more time with friends will go a long way."

He crossed his arms as he digested that bit of information. "Have the kids her age been coming to the café this summer?"

"Yes, some."

"Can Chels hang out with you one day this week?"

Oh, I don't think so was pushing at the edge of her lips. But the earnest look on his face snapped her lips tightly closed. Instead, she uttered, "Of course. How about tomorrow?"

The strong, rugged man smiled, his nearly-black eyes beaming in the moonlight. He took hold of both her hands and gave a quick squeeze. "I appreciate your help."

What on earth was she doing? She should run in the other direction. She didn't have any business taking a middle school girl under her wing. Chelsea was right about the age Ben had been when he started rebelling. Her kid with all A's had done an about-face and had started on the slippery slope toward becoming a juvenile delinquent. And by the time Faith realized what was happening, she'd been too late to stop it.

What if Faith failed with Chelsea, too? What if her advice to Gabe backfired?

"I'll bring her by during my lunch break tomorrow," he said. "If that's okay with you."

"Sure. Anytime."

"Good night, Faith."

His warm, deep voice brushed along her nerves, almost like a brush of his hand, soothing her.

He was a kind man. A good father. A strong leader in the community.

But he was hurting. Probably still grieving. Struggling with a strong-willed daughter.

Okay, so it looked as if God may have put Faith in a position to help father and daughter. She would do what she could. But she better not fail this time.

Chapter Two

Gabe couldn't resist. The next afternoon, a couple of hours after he dropped off Chelsea and traded cell phone numbers with Faith, he cruised by the coffee shop in his squad car and tried to get a glimpse of Chelsea, to see how it was going. Maybe buying her a cell phone with the stipulation she check in regularly wasn't such a bad idea after all.

Ever since Chelsea hit middle school, she'd been begging for the chance to stay home alone. And the previous Friday, he'd actually set the rarely used alarm system and left her alone. But it had been the longest two hours of his life. *What if she falls…or burns herself or a stranger comes knocking?*

Letting her hang out at the coffee shop was only marginally better.

He yanked out his cell phone and dialed Faith's cell number.

"She's fine," she said instead of answering with hello.

Apparently, he was predictable. "Thanks. Don't tell her I checked up on her."

Laughter sounded in the background. And not all of it was female. "Your secret is safe," she said over the din.

He wanted to know exactly who was there doing all that laughing—in that bass voice. "Is Chelsea with a boy?"

"Um. Some of her friends stopped by." He sensed a bit of hesitation. As if she hadn't really wanted to give out that info.

"Thanks." He ended the call and parked, even though he knew Faith would take good care of Chelsea. Even though he knew his daughter would think he was interfering with her brief stint of independence.

Because he knew he wouldn't be able to concentrate on work if he didn't investigate.

He nodded and waved to passersby, calling each by name, as he strode down the blistering-hot sidewalk. Gabe's smile held as he opened the door to Faith's Coffee Time Café.

Faith really had a knack for decorating. Since she'd bought the shop a year ago, she'd made the place feel homey and inviting with a couple of groupings of comfy chairs, tables with Mason jars full of fresh flowers, a display case holding mouthwatering pastries, the perpetual smell of coffee and, normally, soft Christian music in the background.

But today, giggling drowned out the music.

When Faith spotted him, her face screwed up into a wince. She made shooing motions with her hand, as if he were some irritating fly buzzing around the place.

He ignored her warning and meandered toward the table, trying to catch snippets of the conversation—all the while eyeballing the boy sitting glued to Chelsea's side.

The kid with flyaway blond hair and freckles seemed way more than friendly. He and Chelsea had separated a bit from the group, were in their own little conversation. He had his arm around the back of her chair and practically had his tongue hanging out of his mouth like some lovesick puppy dog.

"Chels?" Her name cracked across the café, louder than he'd intended.

More-than-friendly boy popped straight up to standing. He looked familiar, like maybe he was one of those troublemaking Pruitt boys. "Hello, sir," he said. But his voice, in the middle of changing, squeaked halfway through the greeting.

Chelsea's two friends—Valerie and Theresa—laughed.

Chelsea didn't. "Dad? What are you doing here?"

"I just wanted to make sure you and Faith were doing okay."

"We're fine." She stared him down, anger narrowing her eyes and making her face splotchy red.

Too bad. "Well, I'm not sure this was such a good

idea." He gave a nod of his head toward the boy. Then, to Chelsea, said, "It might be time to go."

"I'm just hanging out with some friends from church. I don't want to leave."

Her ramrod straight back probably matched his at the moment. She might look like her mother with her light brown eyes and long, curly hair, but he could only blame himself for her stubborn streak.

They stared at each other in a face-off.

"Good grief," Faith mumbled as she approached the table. "You two are certainly cut from the same cloth."

Gabe glanced at Faith. "I think it's time to break up this little party."

"I'll leave, sir," the boy beside Chelsea said, the *sir* coming out an octave higher.

"Which Pruitt are you?" Gabe barked.

"Parker, sir." The kid was terrified. Acted like he thought he would be arrested for talking to the chief's daughter.

If only it were that easy.

"Gabe..." Faith's sweet, conciliatory tone was wasted on him.

They were talking hormones here. Male and female in close proximity. Male and *his daughter* in close proximity. "Time to go, Chels. Tell your friends bye."

"Chief Reynolds," Valerie said. "Please let her stay. My mom just ran to pick up a prescription. She'll be back in a few minutes."

"I better go," blurted the young Pruitt boy.

About time he took the hint. The boy couldn't get out the door fast enough.

Good. Maybe he wouldn't come back.

Chelsea snatched up her purse and stormed out of the café not far behind Pruitt.

Faith shook her head, then walked over behind the counter. As if he'd failed some test.

He followed her there and he couldn't help but notice how good she smelled. Like last night only with the added sweetness of the pastries. And the coffee. All his favorite smells. "Why are you looking at me as if I'm the villain here?"

She got right in his face and whispered, "You knew she'd be safe here with me. Why'd you have to embarrass her and ruin her fun?"

"Because she's too young to be sneaking off with boys."

Faith's mouth fell open as a *huff* whooshed out. "She didn't sneak off. The others decided to come—as a group, I might add—once they found out Chelsea was here."

"And how did they know she was here?" He drummed his fingers on the counter. "That Pruitt boy—"

"Parker."

"Those Pruitts are bad news. Parker had his arm around her. He was practically drooling on her."

Faith glanced at Valerie and Theresa. "I was watching every move, ready to step in. Nothing inappropriate happened." She snapped a paper towel off the roll and wiped something off the counter. "You asked me to watch her and now you don't trust my judgment."

Great. Faith was trying to help him, and he'd made her—and his daughter—mad at him in one fell swoop.

"Look, I'm sorry. This is new territory."

With a white-knuckled grip, she attacked a coffee ring on the counter. "I understand. You better go check on her."

He'd really blown it. He tried to smile as he threw his hand up in a wave and walked out. When he got to the squad car and saw Chelsea inside in a heap of misery, a wave of regret plowed into him.

He climbed in quietly. "Chels, what's wrong?"

She laughed even as she sobbed. "You're kidding, right?"

He had no clue how to *kiss it and make it better* these days. They were well beyond that stage.

Pitiful black-tinged tears spilled over her reddened cheeks.

"You broke the rules and wore mascara again."

Without acknowledging him, she turned her back and huddled against the passenger door. "Get me out of here before someone sees me."

He drove home slowly, missing his normally cheerful child. As they walked inside the empty house, he tried to put his arm around her shoulders and give her a quick squeeze. She jerked away from him and ran to her room, slamming the door hard enough to rattle the windows.

The ensuing silence roared in his ears. He couldn't stand it, so he turned on the television. Which didn't help much. One of the things he missed most about Tina was the way she'd filled the house with music. She either sang or played the radio all the time.

He looked around the living room. Same paint. Same furniture. Same books and photos. Everything arranged the way it had been the day she died.

But nothing was the same. Never would be again.

And now Chelsea was trying to grow up. He was in over his head and couldn't see how he would manage.

He snapped off the TV and reached in the game cabinet. Maybe a friendly game of Chelsea's favorite, Monopoly, would help smooth things over. He could call Fred to cover for him and take an hour off work.

He carried the game box to Chelsea's room and knocked.

"Go away."

"Come on, Chels. Open up for a sec."

She unlocked the door but didn't open it.

He went inside and found her sprawled sideways, face down, on the pink-draped canopy bed—her little-girl bed. The covers were all bunched up near her head as if she'd dived across the surface, scrunching them up as she slid.

He would not apologize for protecting her. She might not understand now, but she would someday when she had kids of her own. "Come on. Let's play a round of Monopoly."

"No."

"I promise not to win."

She sniffed. "You can't promise that."

"I promise not to put houses on my property." She paused and he thought he had her.

"No, I need to work on my summer reading project."

The paper she'd written two weeks earlier? "I thought you finished it."

"I'll check it over again."

She wanted to check over a project that wasn't due for three more weeks? Boy, he'd sure moved down on her list of fun people. "Okay. I'll let you study."

"You've got to work anyway."

Why did she always say that as if he were committing a crime by holding down a job that provided for her? "I do have a split shift today. Gotta go back from seven to ten. But I can get Fred to cover for a little while."

"So I've got Kristy coming over to stay with me?" Her sneer was no reflection on the babysitter.

"I know you want to stay alone. But not at night. Not yet."

She swiped the back of her hand across her eyes, then sat up. "Well, if you won't let me do that yet, the least you can do is let me go back to the café."

More than anything, he wanted to be a good dad. To keep her safe—physically and emotionally. Maybe this was one little thing he could bend on, though. "Can you promise me no boys?"

"I didn't invite him today." Her gaze darted away. "Well, not directly."

"Is Parker your boyfriend?" He waited for her answer, holding his breath, wishing this day hadn't come.

She shrugged. "No. We're just talking."

This boy-girl stuff was something Tina would have handled so much better. He sat down beside Chelsea on the bed and rubbed her back. "When a boy has his arm around you like that, then it looks like he considers you his girlfriend. Do you want to be his girlfriend?"

"Sort of. Maybe." The sparkle in her eye, though, told him it was a definite yes.

"You need to make up your own mind and not be pushed into anything. Boys, well, they…sometimes they're…pushy." His face must've been as red as hers. He knew they needed a birds-and-bees talk at some point, but—

"I've had health class, Dad, if that's what you're trying to get around to."

He vaguely remembered signing a permission form. "Okay. Good." But he still might need Faith to talk to her.

"Everything is fine with Parker. I like him."

Tina had always prayed for Chelsea. That God

would be working in the life of the man she would marry someday. That God would protect Chelsea and prepare her to meet her future husband. But Gabe had failed to take over the duty, and now something—guilt—nudged him to at least consider praying for his child. But would God even listen to him anymore? It had been so long…" Chels, I don't like this boyfriend-girlfriend stuff at your age. I want you to wait until you're older."

"How old?" Fire lit in her eyes as she challenged him.

Twenty-five? "We'll figure it out later."

He'd been spoiled. He realized that now. He had been Chelsea's whole world the last few years. But now she wanted to broaden her horizons, to include others.

He wasn't ready yet to let her grow up. And though he couldn't stop her, he was determined not to let her rush it.

That evening, when they had a rare moment without a customer at the cafe, Faith sat at a table with Natalie—hardworking, honest, dependable and fun. The best employee she'd ever hired. She thanked God for her every day.

"Since I'll be on vacation for two weeks, you'll need to order supplies." Faith handed Natalie a file folder. "Here's the checklist I use. On Sunday evening after you close, you'll need to do inventory. Then Monday morning, place the orders."

Once they looked over the list together, Natalie seemed confident. "I've got it. No problem." She closed the folder, handed it back to Faith, then slapped her hand flat on the table.

She was acting so strangely. "What—" Faith caught a glimpse of…*a ring?* Natalie had a sparkling diamond ring on her left ring finger. "What on earth?"

The young woman's grin widened. Her eyes radiated joy as she trilled out a happy laugh. "I didn't think you'd ever notice!"

"You and Vince got engaged?"

"Yep. Last night." She wiggled her fingers out in front of her, the diamond flashing in the light.

Faith examined the ring closely. "It's beautiful. Have you set a date?"

"Not yet. Now, back to earth. I've gotta go make the last batch of cookie dough."

Faith resisted the twinge of envy. She'd never experienced the thrill of an engagement or a traditional wedding. Her marriage to Walt had been a quick, hushed trip to the courthouse accompanied by grim-faced parents. And she'd long ago given up on ever finding Mr. Right. Besides, Natalie had snatched up the best man around, even if he was ten years too young for Faith.

There's also Gabe. The thought popped into Faith's mind as she headed to her office to catch up on some paperwork. Yeah, he was a good man, too.

But everyone knew he would never be able to care

for another woman like he had Tina. Though Faith had never met Gabe's deceased wife, she'd heard over and over from friends at church what a paragon of womanhood she'd been. The perfect wife, perfect mother.

And *perfect* was not something Faith could ever do.

As she plunked into her chair, the phone rang. Gabe.

"I feel like I'm imposing on our friendship," he said, "but I'm in a jam. Babysitter canceled last minute and Chelsea suggested I call you."

She closed her eyes. She'd done her neighborly duty—had kept her promise to Chelsea. Had even agreed to help Gabe by having Chelsea come to the cafe that day. But babysit? "I'm here until closing tonight, Gabe. I'm sorry."

"That's okay. I'll keep trying to find someone. Thanks, Faith." He hung up.

She tried not to fret about letting him down, but she did feel a pinch of guilt. Monday nights weren't very busy. And Natalie could probably handle it by herself. Faith could even come back after watching Chelsea and close up.

She smoothed her fingers over the desktop. Everything was in its place—as usual. But she straightened the pencils in the pencil holder anyway, trying to force them to stay evenly spaced around the container.

No. She would not get involved. Gabe could find someone trustworthy to take care of his child. Scads of women from church would love to watch Chelsea.

Gabe fought disappointment after he hung up the phone with Faith. He sensed there was more to her refusal than simple busyness. "Come on, Chels. How about you ride with me for a while? If I get any calls or don't find someone to watch you before your bedtime, I'll call Fred."

"Faith couldn't do it?"

"No. And everyone I tried is tied up at the moment."

Her eyes lit up. "Cool. I'll be ready in a sec."

"You're not going on any calls with me. So don't get your hopes up."

She hurried to her room, then reappeared about ten seconds later wearing pink flip-flops. "Ready!"

The child was entirely too excited about going to work with him. Other than the occasional speeder or fender bender, he didn't have many calls on weeknights. Corinthia was a peaceful little town and he intended to keep it that way.

They climbed in the car and patrolled downtown. The recent renovation of Main Street had given it a much-needed face-lift. New paint, new awnings, pots overflowing with flowers, all made it fresh and inviting.

Most businesses had shut down around five. But a few remained open—the pizza place and Faith's coffee shop among them. Even at seven o'clock, the summer sun and the muggy heat zapped everyone out on the streets. Life seemed to move like molasses in July and August.

Gabe waved to everyone he drove by. Out of the corner of his eye, he noticed Chelsea did the same.

It reminded him of when she was a toddler and used to sit perched in her car seat in the back of his cruiser and wave every time they passed someone—flapping her little fingers toward herself.

Those were the days. Back when he thought he and Tina would have a lifetime together. When he thought nothing bad could touch him again.

Chelsea pointed across the street. "Look, Coffee Time's still open. I'd love some hot chocolate."

"You're kidding. It's ninety-two degrees out."

"Let's stop and see Faith. Please?"

Why did his daughter have a sudden interest in their next-door neighbor and her coffee shop? "I guess. Nothing much going on around town right now."

When they walked into the café, Faith hopped up from a table where she sat with Natalie. When she saw it was them, her smile wilted. She was obviously still mad at him.

He nodded their direction. "Ladies."

Faith met them behind the counter. "Didn't you find anyone to watch Chelsea?" She appeared distressed at the notion.

"No. But we're having a nice time patrolling."

Chelsea grinned up at him. "I'm a good deputy."

Faith brushed some coffee grounds off the counter, then grabbed a towel to wipe up a spot he couldn't see. "I'm so sorry I couldn't help. Natalie and I—"

Gabe's radio squawked. "Excuse me a minute," he said, then he headed outside to take the call.

"Whatya got, Wanda?"

"Possible prowler at the Emersons'," the dispatcher said before rattling off the address. "Empty house. They're on vacation."

"Thanks. I'll head there now." He hustled back inside.

Before he could say anything, Faith held up her hand to silence him. "Go. I'll take her home and watch her and will come back to close up after your shift."

"Are you sure?"

"Positive." She gave him a crooked smile, then waved him away. "Now, go. Go protect your town."

The warmth on her sweet face and in her aqua-colored eyes—and the fact that she was saving his hide at the moment—pierced through his protective gear and right to his heart. A part of his heart that had been cold and dead for a long time.

He locked away the feeling. No time to analyze it, anyway. He had a prowler to catch.

Chapter Three

At nine o'clock that night, Faith sent Chelsea to get ready for bed. But by nine-thirty, she decided to go check on her. She just couldn't imagine the girl having to put herself to bed, even at age twelve.

Chelsea sat on her bed with wet hair, wearing her pj's, with a book in her lap. The stuffed animals and dolls that had most likely graced her bed sometime in the past sat abandoned on a rocking chair in the corner. Somehow, the pink-dotted swiss bedspread and curtains didn't seem to fit, not with the posters of the latest teen heartthrob on the walls.

"Wow, look at you. You're all ready."

"Just call me Miss Responsible. And be sure to tell Dad." She gave Faith a silly wink, then laughed at herself.

"Believe me, I will." She folded the bedspread back to the foot of the bed. "Do you need anything before I tuck you in?"

Chelsea shrugged and looked down at her book

as she twirled hair around her finger. "I don't think so." Her hesitation was just long enough that Faith knew she actually did want something.

"What is it, Chelsea?"

"Well, it's been a long time since anyone dried my hair. Dad's too spastic—gets it all tangled. And I never ask my regular babysitter, because she's usually studying or cleaning the house. And, well..." She continued to twirl strands of wet hair in a circle.

Faith gestured toward the hallway. "Come on. I've never gotten to do the girl-hair thing."

Chelsea's face lit up and she clapped her hands like a young child. She hopped off the bed and raced to the bathroom.

As Faith scrunched Chelsea's curls and blew hot air over them, Chelsea chattered over the loud whir of the motor. "I called Valerie tonight. She invited me to a party at her house—a boy-girl party."

Faith snapped off the hair dryer. "So is this a first, having boys at a party?"

She grinned and nodded. "I hope I can go. Gotta ask Dad."

Faith could only imagine how Gabe would react to this. "Just be sure to find out all the details first. Like, making sure her parents will be home."

"I don't know everything for sure yet. Except that Parker will be there." The last was said in a joyful, singsong voice.

Chelsea could count on the fact her dad wouldn't be happy about that. Faith bit back a smile as she turned the dryer on. Once the hair was dry, she pulled a brush through the silky waves. "There. All done."

Chelsea fluffed her curls. "Nice job. Thanks, Faith." But her interest in her hair was short-lived. She turned away from the mirror and looked up at Faith. "Will you tell my dad about the party for me? It seems like anytime I try to talk to him about anything but studying or church, he goes into cop mode."

Dodging further involvement as mediator, she said, "Like any dad, he loves you and wants you to be safe. To be happy."

"Well, I won't be happy unless he lightens up a little." She walked back to her room and climbed into bed. "I really, really want to do this. And maybe I could even spend the night at Valerie's afterward."

Faith had loved slumber parties. And regular parties—especially the boy-girl variety. In high school, she'd loved to dress up and go to dances, to hang out with friends, to go out on dates.

But then she got pregnant. So she knew all about wanting to socialize yet being unable.

Still, Gabe would understandably be concerned. She sat on the edge of the bed. "I'll mention it to him. But be prepared for a *no*."

"I'm used to hearing *no.* We'll just have to change his mind." She hugged Faith. "Thank you. I'm so glad you came tonight."

Before Faith realized what she was doing, she

kissed the top of Chelsea's head. A motherly gesture she hadn't had the opportunity to do for so long. The sweetness of it pierced her, making her ache in regret for mistakes she'd made. For all she'd lost.

Because of her teen pregnancy and the divorce, she'd tried to protect Ben from making mistakes, which had ultimately driven him away from her. And now it seemed their relationship hung by a thread.

She stood and pulled the covers over Chelsea. "Sleep tight. Don't forget your prayers."

Once Chelsea was tucked in, Faith went to clean the kitchen. But Chelsea and Gabe had done an excellent job already. She couldn't even find a trace of what they'd eaten for dinner. So she busied herself cleaning the toaster.

About the time she finished brushing crumbs out of the little trapdoor and buffing the chrome exterior to a perfect shine, the back door opened, and Gabe walked in. "Hi. She in bed?"

Her heart stuttered. Having him nearby made the room feel two sizes smaller. "Yes. Just a little while ago."

"Thanks. I really appreciate you stepping in."

His grateful smile made her want to turn away, to find something to keep her busy rather than have to look into his penetrating dark eyes. But with the spotless kitchen, she didn't have any option other than facing him head-on—and dealing with this sudden nervousness around him. "So…did you catch your crook?"

"No. I imagine my car ran him off."

Unable to maintain eye contact, she refolded a dish towel and laid it beside the sink. "I have to brag on your daughter. She had showered and was in bed reading when I went back to check on her at bedtime."

He leaned against the kitchen counter. Though he should be proud, he appeared troubled. "She's growing up too fast."

"I know it may feel too fast to you, but I think she's pretty much on target. Other kids her age seem to be facing the same issues."

"Seems all kids grow up too quickly these days." He shrugged. "Anyway, I think going to the café this afternoon was good for her."

"Until you showed up," she teased. Then she grinned at him to ease the jab.

"Yeah, well, she and I had a little talk. If you'll let her drop by again tomorrow, I'll try to keep my nose out of it."

Surely Faith could handle that. It wasn't as if she were committing to raising the girl. And it would be a nice step of independence for Chelsea. "Sure. She's welcome to come back." She stood straighter and forced her attention away from his handsome face. "And while you're feeling generous, we need to talk."

He pulled out the chair and indicated for her to have a seat. "What's up?"

As they sat across from each other at the table, she chose to use an *oh, this is so cute* approach and forced out a laugh. "Well, get ready, Chief Dad. There's more to come."

He leaned on his forearms, all seriousness, not falling for her lighthearted approach. "Suppose you fill me in." His nearly black eyes bore into hers, and she found it difficult to meet his gaze.

"Chelsea has been invited to a party. Her first girl-boy party." She held her breath. Waiting.

He paused for a heartbeat. "No way is she doing that." He frowned for another few seconds, then he relaxed back in his chair. "She's been like a roller coaster all summer. Emotions all over the place. Maybe this liking-boys phase will pass."

"Well, I think she may be hitting the time when she'll start liking them more often than not. Especially when it involves Parker Pruitt."

The frown reformed. "I suppose she does like him. And he'll be at this party?"

Faith wasn't so sure this conversation was going to help Chelsea at all. "She thinks so."

"Chels is not going to any parties."

Faith recognized that determined look on his face. She was fairly certain she'd worn it herself at some point with Ben. "I totally understand. I tried the same with Ben, but it backfired."

"How can doing what needs to be done—the right thing—backfire?"

She didn't know how she could explain without revealing how she'd failed with her son. "I told you, I think being overprotective can be a mistake. So please don't nix the idea without talking to Valerie's parents first. The girl's mother seems very responsible."

He shook his head as he got up from the table, pretty much dismissing her and her ideas.

She followed suit, grabbed her purse off the counter, then opened the door. "I guess I need to get back to the café to finish up."

"Thanks for helping out tonight."

She hadn't come willingly, had done so out of a sense of guilt. But if she were honest, she would acknowledge she'd actually enjoyed herself. "No problem."

He nodded his goodbye. "She'll change her mind about the party, you know. She's not entirely ready to be a teenager. I see glimpses of my little girl all the time."

"Yeah. Maybe so." Faith hated to rain on his parade. But she suspected this time he was in for a surprise.

Late the next morning, Faith left the café and made a quick run to the bank. When she returned through the back door, the dark, rich aroma of coffee greeted her. She didn't think she would ever get tired of the smell, and in some ways, the café felt more like home than her house did. Maybe because the little bit of a social life she enjoyed revolved around work.

And also around church. Although, she often still felt like an outsider. Unless you were born and raised in Corinthia, you weren't truly part of that inner circle that got invited over for birthday parties or Sunday dinner or spur-of-the-moment get-togethers.

She called into the dining room to let Natalie know she had returned. While she washed her hands and put on her apron, she heard Miss Ann's distinctive voice—rather high-pitched and raspy. And very, very Southern.

Miss Ann was a church icon. Whenever townspeople had a problem, they went straight to her for prayer and guidance. And though the woman had lost a lot in her lifetime, she always radiated joy. Always had a kind word. Always wore a smile.

Faith hurried out from the kitchen with an important request in mind. "Hey, Miss Ann."

"I was just praying for you, Faith. Always do whenever I'm near the café."

She patted Ann's shoulder. "And I'm honored that's just about daily."

Ann smiled with rheumy blue eyes the color of an October sky as she held up her mug of hot chocolate—with skim milk and marshmallows—in a mock toast. "Couldn't make it without my daily dose of chocolate."

"Thank you for the prayers. And I have a request for you." Faith pulled out a chair and joined Ann at the small, square table she came to each morning to read her Bible. The carnations in the vase looked a bit ragged, so Faith picked off a browning leaf, straightened them and made a mental note to replace them a day early.

"What is it, dear?"

It wasn't easy to open up and share her worries. But she needed the prayer support, so she took a deep breath and plunged ahead. "I've sort of been thrown into Gabe Reynolds's life the last day or so. I'm trying to help him out a bit with Chelsea."

A grin spread across Ann's face. "You don't say."

"I feel torn. I'd like to help, but I'm so busy here, getting ready for Ben's visit, training Natalie to take over during my vacation. And dealing with a middle schooler..." She hadn't told Ann any more than she'd told anyone else in town, but she hoped the woman would understand her fear. "Please be praying that it goes well all around."

"So is he having trouble with Chelsea?"

"Sort of." She wasn't sure how much to share about his situation. But Ann seemed to be discreet and trustworthy. "Chelsea's growing up. And he's resisting it."

Ann shut her eyes as she grabbed Faith's hand and

held tight with a surprisingly strong grip. She said a short but powerful prayer for Chelsea and Gabe, then she squeezed and let go.

"Thanks, Ann. I guess I better go restock for the afternoon crowd and let you get back to the Scriptures."

As Faith added cookies and muffins to the display case, brought out fresh bags of coffee and refilled the napkin holders, the breakfast crowd dwindled. All except for Ann, who continued to read.

All morning long, every time the door opened, Faith jumped to attention, wondering if it might be Gabe, bringing Chelsea.

At around eleven, they finally walked in. To Faith's dismay, at the sight of Gabe her heart raced and her face burned, scalding her from the inside out. She turned her back to try to gather her wits as she called out, "Welcome. You want your regular, Chief Reynolds?"

"Sure. And a hot chocolate for Chelsea, please." His deep, resonant voice filled the café and seemed to close the distance between them.

"Whipped cream, Chelsea?"

"Yes, please. Oh, hi, Miss Ann!" Chelsea dashed across the dining room and joined Ann at her table.

"Mornin', Miss Ann," Gabe called. He walked toward Faith. As she poured him a cup of coffee and added one packet of sugar, he leaned his thick muscular forearms on the counter and watched her, his intense coffee-colored eyes following her every move.

Why did he always do that? And why did it seem to matter to her more today than it had before?

Another blush wormed its way along her neck and up to her cheeks. Steaming hot coffee didn't help matters any. "Here you go." Once she handed over the cup, she reached under the glass cake stand with a pair of tongs and grabbed several doughnut holes.

He always accepted a bag full even though he complained it would ruin his appetite.

He pulled out his wallet.

"You are *not* going to pay me. Don't try again."

"I don't like it."

"You don't have to like it. You mowed my grass last week before I could get to it. This is the least I can do."

"Just being neighborly. And I still say you're trying to get me addicted to your homemade doughnuts so my car out front will be like an endorsement."

She bit back a smile. "Guilty."

His laugh rang out across the café. "Gotta run. I'll be back for Chelsea in a couple of hours, if that'll work."

"Let her stay as long as she likes. If her friends show up this afternoon she'll want to hang out. We'll either call you when she's ready to go, or I'll run her home."

"Thanks, Faith." He told his daughter and Miss Ann goodbye, then saluted Faith with the bag of doughnut holes as he left.

Once her heart rate returned to normal and her cheeks quit flaming, she carried Chelsea's hot chocolate over and joined Chelsea and Ann.

Ann had closed her Bible and was listening intently.

The girl jumped up and down in her seat when she saw Faith. "Oh, I've been dying to ask. Did you talk to Dad last night?"

"Yes. And I'm afraid he's not going to let you go to the party."

Chelsea sank back in her chair, her face forlorn. "Oh, man. If you can't talk him into it, I know I can't. He's so stubborn. And miserable. I just wish he had something to do besides worry about me."

Ann flipped her notebook open. "I'll add your dad to my prayer list, too."

"Thanks. Pray that he'll finally be happy. It's hard to see him when he gets down, especially at home."

The three of them sat at the table digesting her statement. Faith found herself praying for happiness for Gabe and his daughter. For healing from the grief of loss of such a wonderful wife and mother.

Chelsea sucked in a breath. "You know, I have something else for you to pray about." She had a little gleam in her eye. "Ever since Sunday night, I've been thinking Dad needs something to occupy his time. So—" she signaled for the two of them to lean in closer "—I want y'all to find a bunch of people to be praying for him...to find a girlfriend."

Gabe would be mortified. "Not on the church-wide prayer chain, Chelsea," Faith said.

Ann chuckled. "You sure are a sneaky one, child."

"His whole life is this town and me—specifically keeping me his overly safe little girl. I want him to have some fun."

Faith wasn't sure how she felt about it. Surely it was a good plan. He did need some outside interests. But a girlfriend? On the prayer chain?

She should be all for this. So why did the idea grate against her nerves?

"What do you think, Faith?" Chelsea asked.

"You know your dad won't go along with this. When would he have time to go out?"

"That's the point. He needs to make time. To be *forced* to make time." She grinned at the perfection of her plan.

"How about I add it to my personal prayer list and ask a couple of friends to join in praying?" Ann said as she picked up her cane and slowly got up. "This'll be fun."

Faith wasn't so enthused. All she could think about as she waved goodbye to Ann was that Gabe would be angry. And she would be miserable.

But why would watching Gabe go out and have

fun make her miserable? Did she feel more than a neighborly connection? More than friendship?

No. That was impossible.

"I need your help," Chelsea said, drawing her away from her thoughts.

Faith frowned. "What?"

"We're going to find him a nice woman. Fix him up."

"We are?"

"Yep. And I have an idea for the first one. You!"

"Me?" she asked, entirely too loudly.

"You two have a lot in common—your yards… coffee…church."

"But he doesn't even go to church." Okay, so that was a low blow. The poor man found it difficult to attend without the love of his life. "Besides, we're just friends."

Chelsea shrugged. "Oh. Okay. Well, what about Hannah, from church? We just need to figure out how to get her to ask him out."

Faith's head nearly spun. She hadn't thought of Hannah. But she was perfect for Gabe—and perfect for Chelsea. Hannah was a widowed single mom, a really good mom, always active in her children's lives. A model Christian woman. Gorgeous. "She would be a good choice."

"You know her, don't you?"

"She works at the bank, and I've catered some events for them."

"Perfect! Call her. Tell her to ask Dad out." Chelsea's grin nearly lit the room.

Surely Gabe was going to kill her for this. Then again, he might end up blissfully in love and would thank her. "I'll see what I can do."

"Oh, thank you, Faith! Dad will be so much happier. And I'll be able to live my own life without him worrying about every breath I take."

Faith's stomach seized into a knot. And she could now worry over why she was so resistant to playing matchmaker for her neighbor.

That evening as Gabe took a stroll down Main Street, checking to make sure business owners had closed up tight, he passed two ladies he knew from church walking down the street toward the high school—probably headed for the walking track.

"Evenin', ladies."

"Evenin', Chief," Kendra said, then giggled as if she'd said the funniest thing on earth.

"Got a hot date tonight?" Jeannie asked.

Jeannie wasn't usually someone who teased like that. "Uh…no, ma'am."

"That's okay. Give it some time."

The two laughed as they walked on past.

Strange.

He finished his rounds and headed home. When he walked in the kitchen, Chelsea was setting the table for dinner. Faith was washing pots and pans. Seeing her with her hands in the dish bubbles at his sink brought him up short as a jolt of longing shot through him. A good, I-like-this-scenario jolt.

For a split second, his life felt normal. A brief respite in a rocky five years.

He shook it off and focused on his daughter. The huge grin Chelsea gave him made him want to look over his shoulder to see if the comical Kendra and Jeannie were outside making faces.

"What's up?" he asked them.

"We started dinner," Faith said with her back to him, wiping a dish towel over the outside of a frying pan.

"You have a phone message. I left it on your desk," Chelsea said, and the grin somehow managed to broaden.

He narrowed his eyes. "You sure are cheerful."

"Oh, I'm just excited about the party this Friday."

"Party?"

"Daaaad. You know this info. Faith said she told you."

"Oh, *that* party. Well, you aren't going to any parties with boys."

"I think you'll change your mind." She gave him the happiest, most hopeful grin and batted huge, puppy-dog eyes. Must be some new manipulative tool she'd picked up.

"Chels—"

"Pleeeease...You have to let me. I'll be on my best behavior. I promise. I just *have* to go or I'll be a total outcast."

Talk about exaggeration. "You're impossible." He glanced at Faith, who seemed awfully busy drying the already-dry skillet. "Faith, you sure are giving that pan a work over."

"What? Oh." She looked a million miles away. She pulled her gaze away and placed the skillet in the cabinet. "Time to go home."

He'd thought maybe she felt guilty about encouraging Chelsea over the party. But now he realized she hadn't even been listening to them. She seemed distracted.

After Faith told Chelsea good-night, she headed out the back door to make the short walk next door.

He followed her to the porch and leaned against the railing. "Hey, what's wrong?"

She finally looked directly at him. The glow from the setting sun made her eyes look bluer than usual. Such a pretty color.

She puffed out air that blew her bangs off her face. Then she messed with her ponytail. "I'm just out of sorts. Don't know why."

"I guess Chelsea and I have put an extra burden on you the last few days. I'm sorry."

Her brows drew downward. "No, it's not that at all."

"Then tell me." He motioned for her to sit on the steps beside him.

She started to join him, but then she popped back up. "No, really. It's nothing. I've got to go. And you need to go return Hannah's call." She gave him a crooked smile, then walked away. "Good night."

Hannah? Now why would she be calling?

Must be something to do with security at the bank.

He walked inside to his desk, picked up the sticky note with Chelsea's loopy handwriting, then dialed the phone number she'd carefully written with a huge smiley face beside it.

"Hi, Hannah. Chelsea said you called."

"Oh, hi, Gabe. Thanks for calling back. I, uh… well, this is awkward…but I was…uh…wondering, well…"

"Is something wrong?"

"Would you like to go to dinner this Saturday night?"

Dinner? "Is there something going on at the bank?" He hadn't heard of anything. But he couldn't keep up with every business in town.

A high, bubbly laugh burst out of her. "Oh, I've messed up this whole thing." She laughed again. "I'm trying to ask you out."

Ask him out? "For a bank business dinner?"

"For a date!" she practically hollered, as if trying to get it through his thick skull.

He *felt* thick-skulled at the moment. "A date. You're asking me to dinner as a date? Not something bank-sponsored?"

She chuckled. "I never once mentioned work or the bank. You just assumed."

Surely he'd been tossed into some parallel universe. He didn't go out on dates. And women never asked him out. What was going on?

Chelsea's big grin, her smiley-faced sticky note, Faith's awkwardness...

"Hannah, did someone put you up to this?"

"No. It may have been suggested, but I—"

"My daughter." He would ground her for a month. For a year. And she could forget ever having a cell phone. "I'm sorry, Hannah. I hate that she put you in this position."

"Oh, don't apologize. It seems like a good idea. I just never thought you would consider it."

"You're right. I'm nowhere near ready to date. I'm sorry Chelsea put us in this awkward position."

"Maybe it is time, Gabe," she said softly. "For both of us."

Faith's face flashed into his mind, almost as if *she'd* spoken the words. He shook his head to clear the thought. "I appreciate the offer, Hannah. Maybe another time."

As soon as they hung up, he stomped to Chelsea's room and banged on the door, making the hand-painted name plate bounce and rattle.

"Come in," she said as sweet as sugar.

He marched inside and found her sitting on her bed reading a teen celebrity magazine. "Don't try to get me dates."

"Who, me?" Her face radiated pure innocence from the frilly pink pillow shams.

It was enough to defuse his anger. But embarrassment still made the skin on his face feel a size too small. "Don't be playing matchmaker."

Chelsea scuttled over to the edge of the bed and looked up at him with an innocent expression. Her hair was shiny and her cheeks rosy. "Hannah sure is pretty. And not dating anyone."

"Doesn't matter. Now, behave. Dinner's in ten minutes."

She reached out with her small, soft hand and touched his arm. "Just think about it. You never know what God may have planned for you."

Chelsea's faith—and her ability to talk about it openly—always threw him off balance. But God? What did God have to do with this lark?

He left Chelsea to her magazine and strode to the phone in the kitchen. He hesitated for a second, hand on the receiver, but knew he had to act now. When Faith answered, he said, "You were in on this, too, weren't you?"

"On what?" she asked, almost as innocently as his daughter. "Oh. Hannah's call. Sorry about that."

"I'm not ready for this. And I can't replace Tina, anyway."

Silence. But then Faith sighed. "I know."

For some reason, white-hot anger smoldered beneath the frustration. How could anyone dare to try to fix him up with a woman? "Tina was everything to me. The best wife, best mother. Anyone else would pale in comparison."

Faith was silent. But he could hear her breathing, so he knew she was still there.

"Oh, I'm sure," she finally said with an edge of irritation, almost as if he'd hurt her feelings.

"So please discourage Chels from fixing me up, okay?"

"I'll certainly try. I'll see you tomorrow." She hung up without saying goodbye.

Could he have really hurt her feelings? Had she been as excited to fix him up as Chelsea had been?

Well, it didn't matter. She'd get over it. Besides, there were more important things to deal with than his love life. He had a possible prowler roaming the streets. And it looked as if Chelsea was going to keep badgering him about the party, forcing him to play the mean dad.

He couldn't think about women when he had a town and a daughter to protect.

Chapter Four

Gabe was more than ready to go to work the next morning after listening to Chelsea whine from the moment she woke about having to spend the day with Kristy, her babysitter. Apparently, since beginning summer school, Kristy spent more time studying than entertaining Chelsea.

Now Chelsea had decided Faith was more fun. Well, maybe so, but he couldn't keep imposing on his neighbor.

So he'd settled on giving Kristy money to take Chelsea to Faith's café that day. He felt sure Kristy would do what he asked, but he began to wonder if he'd done the right thing by hiring her that summer, knowing she was enrolled in college courses.

Poor Chels. No wonder she was going stir-crazy.

Gabe tried not to stress about it as he headed to the station. But finding the pastor waiting in his office didn't help. "What can I do for you, Phil?" He gestured for the man to be seated and went around to sit behind his desk.

Phil, who always seemed to be in motion with more on his to-do list than he could possibly fit in a day, sank into the chair and looked at Gabe with tired eyes. "Gabe, I need your help. The kids of the church need your help."

Somehow Gabe didn't like the sound of that. "You know I'm grateful to you and the church for your support. But I don't see how I can help."

"Audra and Gary are moving, and I need new youth counselors. It would give you extra time with Chelsea, too."

He sensed there was more to it than a need for counselors. "So what's the bottom line?"

"I plan to find several workers to share the load. If you could just help me with Sunday-night programs, I'd be grateful."

"And that's it?"

Phil's expression grew serious. "Actually, no. You used to work your schedule so you had Sunday mornings off. I've noticed you work almost every Sunday nowadays. I hope for Chelsea's sake you'll try to go back to the way it was before Tina died."

Of all the topics Gabe had hoped to avoid. His collar suddenly felt too tight. He stretched his burning neck but didn't get any relief. "Well, going to church was difficult after she died."

"I know. It always is in the aftermath. But I think

it's time now. I know Tina would want you to bring her daughter to church."

It was a punch in the gut. And he wanted to defend himself, saying he'd been making sure Chelsea attended. But he knew that wasn't the same. Hadn't he felt guilty every time he dropped her off? *Lord, are You working here—hitting me with this conviction?*

Saying the prayer felt like pushing open a rusty, unused door. But it was good. And a bit of a relief.

A huge sigh escaped.

Phil laughed. "Hard to refuse, huh?"

"You know it is."

"Then do it. Take Sundays off. Attend worship. Work with the youth. I promise the kids will bless you so it won't feel like a chore." He leaned forward and held Gabe's gaze. "You'll be a fantastic role model. Those two Pruitt boys who ride with Chelsea are from a bad home situation. They need a good man to look up to."

Parker, who'd had his arm around Chelsea yet acted polite.

"Nice, Phil. Pull the role-model card, why don't you?"

He shrugged. "Hey, it's just the truth."

And the truth will get you every time. "Okay. I'll try to schedule time off. At least on Sunday evenings for the kids."

Phil stood and slapped Gabe on the back. "Thank you. I knew I could count on you. And hey, if you can work it out, try to come to the youth fundraising dinner next week."

After writing down the details, Gabe said he'd try, then he walked Phil outside.

"I'm sorry if I'm pushing or butting in where I'm not wanted," Phil said. "But I've felt God leading me to talk with you about this."

"I appreciate your honesty. I'll consider what you've said."

He smiled. "Thanks, Gabe. I know you're taking one day at a time. You and Chelsea have come a long way."

"Yeah, we're doing great." If you didn't count how unhappy Chels was with him over the babysitter and the boy-girl party and his forbidding her to wear makeup. And if you didn't count the fact that she was apparently trying to fix him up with a date, as if he couldn't find one for himself. As if he would even *want* to date.

Tina, are you disappointed in how I'm handling everything? You were such a great mom to Chelsea that I don't even know where to start.

"Finally! A moment of peace." Faith waved Natalie over to a large table by the café's front window. The hustle and bustle out on the street always drew her to this spot. "I've pulled everything you'll need for dealing with the banking. Deposit slips. The money bag. And I've made you a cheat sheet so you'll remember what cash you'll leave in the drawer each night."

"Thanks, Faith. Will you show me—"

The front door chimed, indicating a customer had entered. Faith hadn't even seen a car out front. "I guess we'll finish this later."

"Hi," Chelsea called. "This is Kristy. My sitter."

Faith greeted Kristy, a serious blonde who looked as if she didn't have much fun in life. The young woman waved as she headed to a table in the back and plunked an overstuffed backpack on a chair. From the sound of the bag landing, it must've weighed a ton.

Faith raised her brows at Chelsea.

"She's studying for finals. Online summer classes at the community college."

"I see. So what brings you two by?"

Chelsea glanced at her babysitter, then leaned closer. "Dad feels guilty that Kristy's been studying so much. So he gave us money and told us to get out of the house for a while."

Faith grinned at the perceptive girl. "Nice. There's nothing like parental guilt is there?" She slipped her apron over her head and tied it in back. "So what can I get for you ladies?"

"Two medium skinny caramel lattes." She looked proud of herself, almost as if she'd been rehearsing the order.

Faith narrowed her eyes. "Since when do you drink espresso?"

"Since right now. I'd like to try it."

"Somehow I don't think your dad would want you buying coffee with his guilt money."

Chelsea leaned over the counter and rested her elbows on the shiny surface and her chin in her hands. "You can make it decaf if it'll make you feel better."

Clever girl.

As Natalie started their drinks—decaf for Chelsea—the front door chimed once again.

"Well, if it isn't the town's two biggest matchmakers." Hannah approached the counter with a smile on her face. "Hello, ladies."

Faith tried to decipher the smile. Was it the look of a woman satisfied with the knowledge she'd snagged a date with the gorgeous police chief?

"Hi, Miss Hannah." Chelsea beamed at the woman. "Are you and dad going out?"

Hannah, always so loving and motherly, gave Chelsea a quick one-armed hug, then rubbed her back. "No, sweetie. I'm sorry. Your dad said he's not ready to date yet."

A little knot that had been sitting in the middle of Faith's chest loosened. Even though Gabe had fussed at her about matchmaking, she had assumed he would eventually agree to go. How could any man resist Hannah with her sleek black hair and striking green eyes?

Chelsea frowned as she pursed her lips. "Well, maybe he'll change his mind. Just keep working on him."

"I hear I may not be the only one working on him." Hannah nudged Chelsea with her elbow. "I hear you've asked the town to pray for a wife for your dad."

Chelsea's perturbed expression turned to one of hope. "Well, we only asked Miss Ann. But she said she would get a couple of friends to pray."

Faith had a sinking feeling their little trio of prayers had blossomed. "Who's talking about it?"

"Oh, I heard about it from Jeannie."

One of Ann's close friends—who'd probably spilled the beans. "Well, just try to keep it between you ladies. Gabe won't be too happy if he finds out."

"I think it's sweet," Hannah said, "having his precious daughter praying for him to find a wife." She hugged Chelsea once again. "Your dad's a lucky man."

Hannah placed an order for breakfast for an upcoming meeting at the bank, then headed back to work.

For the next half hour, as Kristy drank her latte and pored over massive textbooks, Chelsea sat across from her looking totally bored.

Faith needed to finish up with showing Natalie

how to close the store, but she hated to see Chelsea just sitting there. "Hey, Chelsea, I have a job for you."

The girl's frown instantly turned upward and she jumped into action. "Sure! Anything."

"Um, how about putting out fresh flowers for me?" Okay, so it was two days early. But hadn't she decided to change them soon anyway? "We'll just have to run down to Cricket's to pick them up."

Chelsea hurried across the café toward Faith. Then she looked back at her babysitter. "Kristy, can I go?"

Kristy didn't look up. "What?"

"Can I go with Faith to buy flowers?"

She dragged her attention away from the page. "Um, sure. I guess your dad wouldn't mind."

"We'll be back in fifteen minutes," Faith assured her. Although she wasn't convinced Kristy truly cared.

As they headed out into the hot, humid day, it nearly sucked the air out of her lungs. But Chelsea didn't seem fazed. She chattered as they walked around the downtown square to the other side of the courthouse. By the time they stepped back outside the flower shop with their order, Chelsea had them both giggling like girls.

"What are you two laughing about?"

It was Phil. She'd been so busy howling with laughter she hadn't seen their pastor approach.

"Nothing, really. Just one of those silly moments that catches you off guard."

He smiled at the two of them. "Laughter is good for the soul. And so is prayer. I'm glad the two of you are pulling together the congregation in prayer."

The urge to giggle fled as quickly as it had hit. "Pardon me?"

"Chelsea's prayer request. For Gabe."

"You mean you heard, too?" Chelsea looked very pleased.

No. Don't be pleased. This can't be good.

"Yes. And I'm praying for your dad, too. You're sweet to care so much about his happiness." He wished them a fantastic day as he walked on down the sidewalk.

What if Gabe found out? And what if he thought Faith had something to do with it? "Chelsea, you need to quit asking people to pray for this. Your dad is not going to like it."

"Oh, he won't like it at all. But that's okay."

Faith had a sick feeling she was going to get tied up in a big mess once Gabe found out. She arched a brow at the girl.

"Besides," Chelsea added. "I haven't asked anyone but Ann. It looks like God is doing all the work."

Faith didn't feel one bit of the cheer Chelsea radiated.

But what concerns you more, Faith? What Gabe will think when he finds out...or that God might actually pull this off?

* * *

Gabe tried to check on Kristy and Chelsea later that afternoon. After getting no answer at home, he drove by the café to see if Kristy had followed up on his request. When he walked inside, he spotted the sitter in the back corner.

Studying.

Which didn't bode well for Chelsea's fun outing. "Hey, Kristy. How's it going?"

"Oh, hi, Chief Reynolds."

"Where's Chelsea?"

"She went with Faith to, uh… Oh, man. I can't remember where they said they were going. I'm sorry."

From behind the counter, Natalie called, "They ran to the flower shop. Should be back anytime now."

"Thank you, Natalie." He sat down across from Kristy. "Look, I know you're working hard. I bragged about your ambition just last night. But if you can't handle this job, I need to know."

Tears filled her eyes. "I'm so, so sorry. It's just that my first finals are scaring the life out of me. What if I fail?" The last word practically squeaked out of her. "My mom would kill me. She didn't want me to do this—said I'm not mature enough to keep up in summer classes."

The poor thing. He knew her mom and she was pretty hard on the kid. "How about if I give you next week off?"

"You mean it?"

"Sure. I'll just call you when I absolutely can't find anyone else."

"Yes! Thank you. Call anytime, day or night. And if you need me right then, I'll head over."

"It's a deal." He shooed her and her ton of books toward the door. "Now go on home. I'll get tomorrow covered, as well."

"Bless you." She tossed the thick textbooks in the bag and skittered out the door. A minute later, in walked Chelsea and Faith, loaded with two boxes of flowers, followed by Chelsea's good friend Valerie and her mom, Olivia.

Chelsea spotted him and waved. "We've been over at Cricket's. And you wouldn't believe what happened." She burst out laughing. "I said something about Cricket. And I didn't mean it to be funny. But Faith got tickled. And then we both laughed so hard it hurt. And we had to go outside to get a grip. And then Pastor Phil caught us doubled over, laughing hysterically."

He smiled at his expressive child. She'd always loved to tell a good story. "Sounds like you and Faith had a good time."

Valerie jumped in, waving her arms to get everyone's attention. "Mr. Reynolds, we passed Kristy and she told us she's taking some time off. How about letting Chelsea stay at my house tomorrow?"

"That sure would help—" Tomorrow. *Friday.* "But wait…" He looked at Faith to see if she was thinking what he was thinking.

Chelsea squealed. "Oh, that would be perfect! Please, Dad?"

Faith gave him a sympathetic look, even though she thought Chelsea should be allowed to go to the party. "Chelsea, I'd actually hoped you would hang out here with me tomorrow."

A flash of gratitude made him smile at her. She smiled back with those gorgeous eyes, which sent another flash through him—only this time it wasn't gratitude. It was attraction, pure and simple.

Whoa. Confusion clouded his brain. Faith was making him feel things he hadn't felt in years. Things he couldn't afford to feel when there was no chance of him ever finding perfect love again—especially love he could lose.

He pulled his attention from Faith and focused on his daughter. He couldn't simply let Faith try to bail him out. "Honestly, Valerie and Olivia, I don't feel comfortable allowing her to attend a party with boys."

"I promise it'll be well-chaperoned." Olivia put her arm around her daughter's shoulders. "I've got three grandparents and two sets of aunts and uncles coming to help."

"Oh, *pleeease,* Mr. Reynolds." Valerie was so tense she nearly vibrated. Then she took hold of Chelsea's hand and waited for his answer.

Chelsea's doe eyes nearly undid him. Not because they looked hopeful. Not because they looked pleading. But because they looked resigned, as if she already knew the answer.

"I know you and your family, Olivia. You're trustworthy. But I just can't do it yet."

Pity etched lines in Olivia's face as she patted his arm. "I totally understand. Come on, Val, let's head on over to the grocery store."

Chelsea jammed her hands on her hips. "I won't give up."

"Oh, I almost forgot the reason we stopped by…" Olivia dug in her purse, then came up with a scrap of paper. She put it in Gabe's hand, then closed his fingers over it. "Call her. She'd love to go out."

As Olivia and Valerie left, he looked at the paper. It had a phone number and a name.

Someone he knew to be single and available.

He must seem pathetic to everyone around him—as a father and a man. Enough so that, for some reason, they all suddenly felt the need to try to fix him up.

Chelsea's defiant stance eased. She tried to hide a snicker behind her hand, but he heard it nonetheless.

Faith stared toward the wall. But he thought he saw her shoulders shake.

Finally, Chelsea gave up hiding the fact she was laughing at him. She let out with a full belly laugh. "Sweet."

"I don't see what's so sweet." Still, it was nice to hear Chelsea laugh, and she seemed happier than usual.

"No, Chelsea, this is not funny," Faith said even as

a chuckle welled up from under the stern expression she'd tried to hold.

With hands held up, palms forward, Chelsea said, "I didn't do anything. I didn't say a word to Valerie's mom."

"Then why do random people keep asking me if I have a date and handing me phone numbers?"

"Coincidence?" Chelsea asked.

He glared at his daughter and neighbor, who leaned into each other as if they were the best of buddies.

Well, if it would help them bond, he would let them have their fun at his expense. He liked seeing Chelsea laugh. Liked seeing her interact with a good woman who cared about her.

He watched Faith's profile as she joked with Chelsea. Watched Chelsea's face as it radiated happiness—even after he'd denied her attending the party.

His daughter was happier with Faith in her life.

His gaze was once again drawn to Faith. As she smiled, he fought the sudden urge to trace her lips with his finger, to map that smile.

But images of her lips jumbled with memories of Tina's, and he knew he was treading in dangerous waters.

Chapter Five

"I need the weekend off," Natalie begged Faith on Friday morning. "And Monday, too. I'm so sorry I didn't ask sooner. But Vince and I need to go to Tennessee to tell his family about our engagement before they hear it through the grapevine."

Scattered and a bit frantic already, Faith opened the oven door and pulled out a pan of muffins. "I'm supposed to interview a part-time employee this afternoon—someone to help you while I'm on vacation. What time do you have to leave?"

Natalie winced. "Don't hate me…"

"What time?"

"Now." She grabbed Faith's hands. "I'm so, so sorry. I can't believe I'm doing this to you."

Faith couldn't believe it, either. Natalie had been nothing but dependable since she started working. But she was now engaged. The excitement of a new stage of life and all. "Okay. Go ahead. Have fun. But hurry back as quickly as you can."

"Oh, thank you. I'll be back Monday evening." She threw her arms around Faith and gave her a big squeeze. Then she zipped out the door.

Three days. Without her best employee.

But then the front door opened and Miss Ann entered, and she didn't have time to think about it anymore. Her day had started.

"So, has Gabe found a girlfriend yet?" Ann asked.

Faith made Ann's hot chocolate, then produced a warm blueberry muffin. "He's refused to go out with anyone."

"Well, we'll just have to keep praying that the right woman comes along to help him get over his objections." Ann looked Faith in the eye, almost as if waiting for something.

"Okay." Although, she hadn't yet done her share of praying for Gabe and this new woman who was supposed to make him so happy. Maybe Ann sensed her hesitancy. "Actually, I probably haven't been holding up my end on the praying. I'll try to do better." She handed Ann her mug.

"You're doing a great job helping him with Chelsea."

"I'm trying. But it's difficult. You know, I can't really focus on her right now. I need to be thinking about my plans with my son."

"Oh, we all have plenty of love to share. God's love is limitless."

Why did Ann's words always convict Faith?

Plenty of love to share. Should she try to be less

fearful of messing up and share more of herself with Chelsea? It might loosen her up for her time with Ben.

The thought stuck in her head throughout the busy morning. By nine-thirty, she had a line forming. She couldn't catch up with just one person working.

The cell phone in her pocket vibrated. *Great.* It would have to wait.

By the time she got a chance to check the phone, it was nearly eleven o'clock. She had a voice mail from Chelsea.

Dad still says no. I need your help! I also need a new hairstyle for the party just in case. Please call me!

Okay, she could make a quick call before getting ready for the interview. She also needed to call Ben to wish him good luck in his tournament. And she needed to plan a menu for the week. Plus, a shopping list. She'd be feeding a growing boy—no, a growing man—once again.

First, she dialed the Reynoldses' home number.

"Faith! I'm so glad you called," Chelsea answered.

The excitement in the girl's voice was like a breath of fresh air amidst the chaos of the morning. "Hi. Who's staying with you today?"

"Gretchen from the high school youth group. But she has to leave at noon. Can I come over there and hang with you? I'll help you around the café."

"Oh, Chelsea, Natalie's out of town, and I'm by

myself. Plus, I have an interview scheduled for this afternoon. It won't be any fun."

"That's okay. I'll help you."

How could she refuse when Chelsea was never a bother? "I'll talk to your dad and see if he'll let you."

"Thank you, Faith. And please, please talk to him again about the party. I haven't been able to change his mind. I'm desperate."

She sure hoped she wasn't making Chelsea depend on her too much. "Sweetie, I'm afraid there's no hope there. But I'll try."

After they hung up, she called her son. As usual, she went directly to voice mail.

"Hey, Ben. I just wanted to wish you well in the tournament this weekend. Have a safe trip. And call me to let me know how it's going."

She'd be surprised if he actually did.

"Oh, and by the way, I'm busy making plans for your visit." She tried to get past the hurt of having him repeatedly ignore her calls and brightened her voice. "Let me know any special meals you'd like. Love you. Bye."

She hung up and prayed that God would work to soften Ben's heart toward her, would break down the wall of resentment. And would help her to find the best way to show him love.

As Gabe walked down the street, intent on buying charcoal for grilling out that night, he had a feeling someone was following him. He came to a dead stop and turned.

Someone in a flapping cape nearly ran into him. And a glare from something metal blinded him. He shielded his eyes.

"Wait, chief." A woman huffed, trying to catch her breath. "I've been chasing you from the salon."

The cape was a barber-shop—er, beauty-shop cape. And the metal turned out to be some kind of aluminum foil stacked in the woman's hair like a Rolodex. She smelled like chemical bleach.

He backed up a step and resisted pinching his nose closed. "I'm sorry. I didn't hear you."

She fanned her red face with her hand. "I wanted to make sure you know my Kelli Lyn is free this weekend." She puffed out her chest and smiled. "She's a pretty thing, you know."

It finally hit him who he was talking to. She didn't look a thing like herself with all that goop in her hair. "Uh, yes, Mrs. Hunt. Your daughter is very pretty." And young.

And why on earth would you be telling me this?

"She'd be thrilled if you called her." She gave his arm a squeeze. "Yesiree, you're quite a catch."

"I…uh, thank you."

She leaned in and the bleach fumes nearly burned his nostrils. "We're all praying for you. And I'm honored to be part of it." She spun around, her cape taking a moment to follow suit, twisting around her body. Then she motioned as if putting a phone to her ear. *Call her,* she mouthed.

Surely his daughter hadn't talked to Kelli Lyn or her mother. He didn't even think Chelsea knew them.

Faith.

It had to be Faith who put him in this embarrassing situation. He'd thought he could take the teasing from her and Chelsea. But now it involved more than just a couple of their friends. Now it was getting out of hand. It could ruin his reputation as police chief if no one took him seriously.

He changed direction and stormed across the street toward the coffee shop. It was time to put a halt to this ridiculous matchmaking scheme before one more person heard about it.

He stomped into the café and found Faith sitting at a table with a young woman. Luckily, no one was in line. There were just a couple of patrons at other tables.

He approached Faith's table. "Excuse me just a moment."

"I'm sorry, Gabe. Can this wait about thirty minutes? I—"

"No, I'm sorry. It can't wait. You're butting into my business and I want it to stop."

Her face reddened. "Um, Juanita, this is our police chief, Gabe Reynolds. Gabe, this is Juanita Alvarez, the woman I'm *interviewing* for a possible part-time position. Her family is new in town." It was a wonder

Faith could speak since she was gritting her teeth like a vise.

Interviewing? Oh, man. He'd messed up. "I'm sorry to interrupt. Nice to meet you, Miss Alvarez."

"That's okay. Maybe I should go and let you two talk." She stood and looked at Faith as if concerned, as if maybe she should reconsider working for her. "I'll call to reschedule." She hurried out the door. And he doubted she would actually call.

Faith stood and gripped the table with both hands, looking as if she'd like to bend the thing. "I can't believe you just did that. She was perfect. Has even worked at Starbucks for three years. And you just scared her away."

"I'm sorry. But because of whatever you and Chelsea have been up to, I just had a woman with foil in her hair chase me down the street and try to force her daughter on me."

"What?" She threw her arms out in question. "I have no idea what you're talking about."

"You've overstepped. I understand that you'd contact Hannah. And that Chelsea would contact Olivia. But Mrs. Hunt just chased me down the street, all the way from the beauty shop—with bleach in her hair, no less—and tried to make sure I would call Kelli Lyn to ask her out this weekend. *Kelli Lyn,*" he roared. "She's, like, twenty-two years old." He crossed his arms to keep from pointing his finger at her. "You've overstepped."

Faith looked around the café, then she yanked

him into a chair. She sat down beside him. "First, I never said a word to anyone but Hannah. Second, your daughter simply asked Miss Ann to pray for you. Ann did offer to ask two friends to pray, as well. So I guess that's where all this started."

He dropped his head forward. *Kendra and Jeannie.* This was worse than he thought. "So I've somehow gotten on the prayer chain?"

"That wasn't supposed to happen. But you know small towns. Things take on a life of their own."

Yes, unfortunately, he did know. "Can you call this off?"

"I don't know. But I can try."

"Well, please do. This is humiliating."

"I'll do my best—" she arched a brow at him "—if you'll call Juanita and apologize and beg her to take the job offer I was about to make."

How had he managed to get into these messes? Just a week ago, his life had been perfectly calm and somewhat normal—as normal as can be with a twelve-year-old daughter in the house. "Fine. And look, I'm sorry about barging in like that. I was sure you were responsible."

She waved him off. "It's okay." She jotted Juanita's number on a napkin and handed it to him. "While you're here, we need to talk about the party tonight."

"Chelsea's not going."

She laid a hand on his forearm. "I have a solution.

Go with her. Stay by her side the whole night if you have to. Just don't make her miss it."

How could one small touch make it so difficult to focus? He slid his arm off the table. "I've made my decision. I'm against it on principle. This whole boy-girl thing in middle school is ridiculous."

As she stood and reached for her coffee mug left from the interview, she blew her bangs off her forehead. "Well, I tried."

Though he was probably pushing his luck, he had to act before she got back to work. "I have another favor to ask."

She heaved an exaggerated sigh. "You really are messing with *my* life, too, you know."

He smiled. Because, well, there was just something about her that made him want to. The way she acted put out even when he knew she would do anything to help anyone who needed her.

He touched her hand to stop her from picking up the second mug and walking away. It was slightly work-roughened and warm—which reminded him of Faith at his kitchen sink. "Since Kristy is taking a break, can I impose on you to watch Chelsea on the evenings when I have a split shift, working seven to 10:00 p.m.? Just for a week."

She looked down at where his hand rested on hers. Then she let go of the mug and drew away. "Natalie is out of town this weekend, so I'll be here long hours. But next week should work out okay." She clenched the hand she'd pulled away, then reached for the mug once again. "Of course, Chelsea offered to help me this weekend. I guess she could just hang here and I could let her wipe tables and answer the phone."

Why did he always feel warmed inside when she agreed to help him? Of course, she could warm him even if she refused. She was really starting to get to him. "That sounds great. She'd love it. And maybe it would take her mind off missing the party."

A grin, or rather more of a snarl, lifted one corner of her upper lip. "Yeah, nice. Make me be the one who has to deal with the fallout of preteen-girl angst."

He shoved his hands in his pockets, feeling lighter than he had in ages. A stupid grin pasted itself on his face. "What are neighbors for?"

She punched him in the arm, but it was gentle, teasing. "Go on. Bring Chelsea to me whenever you need to. We'll figure it all out somehow."

"Thanks, Faith. I owe you." He left the café, bought the charcoal and then headed home. Time to break the news to his daughter about the party. But the consolation prize of hanging out with Faith might soften the blow.

"Why can't you be normal?" Chelsea whined, her lip wobbling as she fought tears after his final refusal to let her attend the party. "I'll miss everything. And what if Parker decides he likes someone else?" She huffed in a big breath, but it caught in her chest, making the sound of a miserable sob.

So much for softening the blow. "Well, if he does, then he wasn't worth liking." Gabe nodded to accentuate the sound advice he was giving, absolutely certain Tina would say the exact same thing.

Chelsea threw herself on the bed. "Oh, Dad, you are so clueless." Another sob tore through her as she began to cry for real. "You've ruined my life."

When he sat beside her and tried to soothe her by patting her back, she jerked her shoulder blade to shake his hand off. Instead, he ran his fingers through her hair like her mother had always done and she didn't object.

Her long, silky curls reminded him of Tina's hair, which he loved so much. "I have a nice surprise for you."

"Just leave me alone." Her muffled wail sounded through the room.

Not the type of sound he wanted filling their home. He wanted brightness and joy again. Music, laughter, chatter, the click-clack of high heel shoes across the wood floors.

The sound of bacon frying, the hand mixer signaling the baking of a cake.

Everything was so horribly quiet.

Except for the crying jags he caused. "Honey, I know I can't fill your mom's place. I miss her, too."

A growling sound welled up from deep within her

as she reared up onto her knees. "No, I don't miss her," she screamed in his face. "I miss *you*."

He recoiled. As her statement echoed through the pink frilly bedroom then faded, the gut-kick pain throbbed on.

She missed him?

Though the comment made no sense at first, he soon realized what she meant. And she was right.

When Tina had breathed her last, she'd taken a piece of him with her.

The good part of him.

He'd grown up in a totally dysfunctional family. Couldn't get away from them fast enough. And then Tina had come along. Sunshine, sweetness—she'd given him hope that good things could happen. That there really were good women out there who could love their husbands and children and take care of them. And he'd wanted to be a part of that beauty.

Now the product of their beautiful love was suffering because he'd been mired in grief.

He squeezed his eyes shut, trying to hold back the pain. *God, I've been trying to do this alone for so long. Please help me.*

He tried once again to rub Chelsea's back. This time, he held on when she tried to buck him off. Finally, she gave up.

A moment later, she threw herself into his arms. "I'm sorry, Daddy. I didn't mean it."

He patted her heaving shoulders until her crying

eased. "It's okay, baby. You're right. I've not been there for you like I should."

"No, it's not that. It's that you've changed. I miss the fun, happy you." She pulled back and looked him in the face, her eyes red and soggy and swollen. "Actually, you've been there for me a little too much lately." She smiled through the tears, wiping her eyes with the back of her hand.

He gave her a crooked smile in return as he shook his head. "Well, a dad can't help being protective. Especially when he's lost his parenting partner."

"You'll do okay by yourself if you'll just give me a chance to grow up."

But then I'll be totally alone.

The thought brought him up cold. He'd never acknowledged it before. Didn't want to now.

Dread tried to choke him. He forced himself to quit thinking of a future he couldn't control and focused on the present. His daughter wanted some independence. Surely he could manage a simple step toward letting go.

He gave her shoulder a gentle squeeze. "It's hard for me to let you grow up, because I've realized more and more it'll just be me around here. I guess that's why I'm trying to slow the process."

"I thought you were just being stubborn."

"I only want what's best for you, Chels."

She gave him a tentative smile as she pressed his face between her warm hands. "And I want what's best for you. So…"

He knew what was coming. It involved dating. "Hey, Faith offered to let you come help her this weekend. Your first job."

She raised a brow as if she knew exactly what he was doing. "Okay…"

"You'll be able to help her some while Natalie's out of town. No pay, of course. But if you do a good job, I'll give you extra allowance."

She crossed her arms and flopped back onto the bed. "But I'm still stuck here while everyone is at the party tonight."

"Come on." He got up and headed toward the door. "I'll go call the young woman Faith interviewed today and see if I can convince her Coffee Time Café would be a great place to work. Then let's have that cookout I promised you."

She replied with a whine, softened with a smile. "And afterward, I'll beat you at Monopoly."

Sometimes his love for Chelsea nearly overwhelmed him. It hit him once again as he accepted her challenge. He just hoped his love was enough.

Faith loved waking early before the sun had a chance to weigh the air down in oppressive heat. Birdsong and fresh, dewy green grass greeted her as she headed to her car at five-thirty on Saturday morning. When she arrived at the café, she found Gabe and Chelsea on her doorstep. "Wow, you two are up early."

Chelsea looked only partially awake. She rolled her eyes.

"Early shift," he said. "Thanks for letting her hang out and help."

Faith unlocked the door and motioned them inside. Chelsea shuffled through the kitchen and into the dining room and sank into one of the comfy chairs.

"You look bright and chipper this morning," Gabe said as he examined every feature on her face.

"I've been up awhile. Working on a shopping list for Ben's visit."

"Do you need any help?"

She waved away his offer. "Thanks. But once I hire someone, I should be okay." She angled her head toward the dining room. "Now come on in and get some coffee and something to eat before you head to work."

A smile transformed his face from the usually serious cop look. "That sounds nice. Someone to make me breakfast. And, by the way, I called Ms. Alvarez. I think she'll take the job."

What a relief. "Thank you." She pulled together a breakfast of pastries and fruit for the three of them. *What I wouldn't give to have someone to make breakfast for every day. To eat meals with, too.*

An ache that plagued her from time to time struck once again. With a vengeance. But Ben would be coming soon, and she would have her son to cook for. To spend time with.

"Ben's in a baseball tournament this weekend," she told them as they finished eating. "His traveling team has been really successful this summer, although he said he doesn't think they have any chance of winning this one."

Chelsea dunked the last bite of her doughnut in her hot chocolate. "Do you ever go watch him play?"

"Whenever he plays in the Atlanta area, I try to go see at least one or two games a week. But they've been on the road a lot lately. To places where college scouts are hanging out."

"Exciting stuff," Gabe said.

"Yeah, I just wish…"

"What?"

"That I could be there for more games. He'll be graduated and gone before I know it."

Gabe tipped his head toward his daughter. "Tell me about it."

Chelsea snorted. "Yeah and I'll be the only college student who's never spent the night away from home or attended a boy-girl party."

"Or has a cell phone," he added as he ruffled her hair. Then his touch gentled, and he pushed her hair behind her ear. "There's no hurry. Take your time and enjoy being a kid."

The tender gesture gave Faith a jolt the equivalent of about two cups of strong, fully-leaded coffee.

Chelsea rolled her eyes at him.

He slapped his legs and stood. “Gotta run. I’m late. You two have fun.”

Faith tried not to stare as he lumbered out. Tried not to notice how his uniform shirt clung to broad shoulders and tapered to narrow hips. Tried not to think about how strong and capable he was.

She’d thought that about her ex-husband in high school, too. He’d been the strong football player, confident and charming. And without a dad at home, she’d eaten up the attention from a big, take-charge kind of guy.

But once they married and moved to campus so he could attend college, he found college life too fun to resist. And responsibility for a pregnant wife too odious a task.

He resented her even as she worked to help pay for his tuition. Then not long after Ben was born, he’d come home drunk one night—reeking of some sorority girl’s perfume—and told her he wasn’t happy and wanted a divorce.

She heaved in a deep breath and tried to keep the sigh to herself. What would it be like to wake up beside someone like Gabe every morning? To know he would always be there to love, honor and protect her.

A silent, mocking laugh rang through her mind. Who was she kidding? No one was ever there for always. Even a good man like Gabe couldn’t promise forever.

“Come on, Chelsea. Let’s get to work.”

They set up for the business day. Faith handled the morning rush fairly well while Chelsea wiped tables and answered the phone. By the time Miss Ann showed up, later than usual, it was the perfect time for a break.

The three of them gathered around Ann's regular table.

Ann patted her prayer notebook. "So, Chelsea, dear, how's it going with your dad? Has he found Miss Right yet?"

"Found?" Chelsea was incredulous. "Are you kidding? The women are finding *him*. But he's ignoring them."

"I think we need to call off the prayer request." Faith bit the inside of her cheek, hating to disappoint Chelsea. "He's starting to get frustrated. I mean, Mrs. Hunt chased him down the street yesterday with foils in her hair, trying to fix him up with Kelli Lyn."

Chelsea giggled.

"I bet that was a sight," Ann said. "Unfortunately, there's nothing I can do. I only told Jeannie and Kendra, but apparently, word leaked out. In fact, I just opened an email from another of my prayer loops asking me to pray for Gabe to find a wife."

Faith wanted to bang her head on the table. Poor Gabe. "Which loop?"

"From a church over in Athens. The ladies thought it was so sweet that a little girl wanted to find a wife for her grieving daddy. I bet they've forwarded it all over the country by now."

For some reason, the thought hit Faith as totally hilarious. Laugher bubbled up and out despite her fears over his anger. "Oh, my. Gabe's plight has gone viral. Thank goodness no one has his email address, or he'd be getting proposals from women all over the country." Especially if they knew what a catch he was.

Chelsea joined in the laughter. "I think it's great. He can have a date every night of the week. Surely he'll fall for one of them."

Miss Ann grew serious. "Ladies, I think we may need to modify our prayers." She opened her notebook, flipped through the pages, then started to write. "Let's pray that with all these prospects, Gabe will only pick the right woman for him—and right for you, too, Chelsea. Let's pray that he'll know when he's found God's choice for him."

Faith's face and ears burned. *Lord, why is this always so upsetting for me to think about?*

It wasn't as if some woman would be able to fall in and take Tina's place. He'd said so himself. No matter how wonderful, no one could fill those shoes. Even as perfect as Hannah was, Faith had a feeling Gabe would never see her as good enough.

So why does this bother me? Am I carrying some insane urge to have him notice me?

"Faith?" Ann asked.

"Okay, I'm in." She rubbed her apron over a

smudge on the table to bring it to a perfect shine. "I'll pray for Gabe to fall for the woman God wants for him."

Chelsea rolled her eyes. "Well, I'm not so picky. I'm still just praying he'll find a girlfriend to date so I can have a life."

They all broke out laughing at Chelsea's wish.

But Faith's insides were jumbled, conflicted. Could she really pray for this and mean it? What if God brought someone new into Gabe's life? Could she be happy for him?

It was crucial for her to be able to do that. Because if she couldn't, then it meant she was falling for him. Which was crazy.

Of course she wasn't falling for him. She was merely attracted to him. And enjoyed being around him. No big deal. That could happen with any nice, handsome man. *Lord, help me pray this and mean it.*

Help me to have faith in You and Your plan.

Antsy, she jumped up, looked around at the empty café and decided she had to have a distraction. "Let's close for an hour and do something fun."

"Feeling spontaneous, huh?" Ann asked. "I like that. You need some freedom from all your responsibilities."

"Let's go shopping," Faith said. "I could use a new pair of work shoes."

"How boring," Chelsea said after checking out

Faith's comfortable walking shoes. "I have a better idea. Let's go get a makeover."

"A makeover? In an hour?"

"Well, I want a new hairstyle. Let's get our hair done. Dad will pay you back."

Ann begged off, claiming a doctor's appointment, and headed out. Faith was just about to back out and be sensible when she noticed how dejected Chelsea looked.

The girl worried with the edge of her mug. "You're afraid to leave the shop, aren't you?"

How could she deny Chelsea a new hairstyle? She had begged for one yesterday, for the party. And then she'd been forbidden to go. Maybe this could be the consolation prize. "Okay." She pulled her apron off and scribbled a note for the front door. "Let's do it."

Chelsea lurched forward and hugged her. "Thank you. I feel special."

"You *are* special. Now…nothing drastic at the hair salon, okay?"

"I have something in mind. Nothing drastic. Besides, it's only hair. It'll grow back."

Chapter Six

That afternoon as Gabe was walking toward the diner to grab a bite to eat for a late lunch, he noticed two ladies walking down the sidewalk in the opposite direction on the other side of Main Street. He nodded a polite hello, and was about to push the diner door open, when something about the way they walked nudged him into stopping.

They walked like—

"Hey, Dad!" Giggling followed the greeting from the shorter *lady* across the road.

His gut clenched. *No way.* He squinted and tried to focus as they crossed the street toward him. "Chelsea?"

She grinned. "Of course."

Faith held back, approaching more slowly. She looked different, too. But not as different as his daughter.

Any thought of lunch fled as he stared at Chelsea's

short, choppy hair. "Your hair..." The gorgeous curls. Gone.

She smiled and twirled in a circle. "Do you like?"

No, he didn't like. And she didn't resemble her mother anymore. "You look like me," he said dully.

"I know. Isn't it weird?"

She was so happy and he didn't know how to react. He glanced over at Faith, who looked amazing. "What happened?"

Faith shrugged and had the decency to look sheepish. "We got new hairstyles."

Chelsea stepped protectively in front of Faith. "It was my idea. I begged her to take me to get my hair cut."

How could they have left him out of such a big decision? "It doesn't matter who suggested it. You should have asked me first."

"I like it," Chelsea said with her chin raised and shoulders back. "I'm tired of not being able to style my own hair." Even with her bravado, tears popped up in the corner of her eyes. "And now you ruined our fun."

"I'm sorry, Chels. It's just a shock. You look so much older."

That seemed to pacify her. She smiled through the tears. "Good. And Faith looks young and hip."

Faith's hair did look nice. The ponytail was gone. The style was still long, but seemed to have more layers and waviness to it. But then again, she was pretty all the time. "Yes, she looks nice." *What an understatement.*

But that didn't change the fact Chelsea had totally changed her hair without permission and now looked sixteen. "Chels, go on back to the café. We'll catch up after I talk to Faith for a minute."

Chelsea took Faith's proffered keys and headed quickly toward the shop.

He jammed his hands in his pockets. "How could you let her do something so outrageous?"

"It's not outrageous. Besides, I didn't know she would get so much cut off. She told me she wouldn't do anything drastic."

"And you left a twelve-year-old on her own to decide?"

She appeared dumbstruck, then blurted, "She looks cute."

"She looks grown. Guys will be staring at her now."

"She just wanted something more practical, and to do something fun."

How could Chelsea's looking like her mom—then suddenly not looking like her—upset him so? *It's another loss.*

Unable to explain his reaction to Faith, he turned and walked toward the coffee shop.

Faith's footsteps sounded from behind him. When she caught up to his long strides, she grabbed his arm. "Don't give her such a hard time. It's just hair. It'll grow back."

"It's not just hair. Tina loved Chelsea's hair. She used to brush it every night. She dried it after every washing." He swallowed a hard knot of grief. "Chelsea looked like her mother. And now…" He waved his hand toward the door of the café.

It was like losing a little more of Tina when he was trying so hard to hang on to the memories. To cling to a time when all had been right in his world. Drained of energy, he didn't even try to explain it further.

Faith stepped in front of him and put her hands on his arms. "I'm so sorry. I had no idea."

He fought to get a grip. To check his emotions. Because he knew he was being ridiculous. "Hey, no big deal. At least it shouldn't be, anyway."

"Well, apparently, it's more of a deal than I realized." She huffed in frustration as she reached for a ponytail that wasn't there. Then she blew her bangs off her forehead—a gesture that was becoming familiar.

He pushed her bangs to the side for her. She was so close. And was touching him. And it hit him how much he missed physical contact. Contact with someone soft and sweet and who smelled so good.

She stepped away, as if his touch had frightened her. "Again, I'm sorry. I should have known, well…the thing with her looking like Tina." She shrugged. "I just thought it was one way you could give her some independence. She was so frustrated over the party, I was afraid she might do something rebellious."

An irrational fear. She had mentioned it several times. Maybe it was time to give her a chance to explain. "How did Ben rebel?"

She sighed and shook her head. Then she leaned against the storefront window and stared off into the distance, as if lost in the past. "In middle school, he started hanging with the wrong crowd. He quit studying. His grades hit rock-bottom." She threw her hands out helplessly. "He just checked out. Nothing I said reached him."

He wanted to touch her again, but he didn't dare. "I'm sorry."

"It's all in the past. And he's fine now." She smiled, but he wasn't so sure all was truly fine. The smile didn't seem genuine. Something still bothered her.

"So if all's well, why do you worry so much about his visit?"

Her shoulders sagged as if some invisible weight pushed on them. "Honestly, he's angry at me all the time, and I don't know why. He's avoided visiting ever since he got his driver's license. And I'm afraid he'll cancel this visit at the last minute."

He had no idea what to say. He hadn't known she'd been struggling so.

"Sorry. I didn't mean to dump all that on you." She turned and grabbed the café door handle.

He put his hand on her arm to stop her. "Don't apologize. I'm glad you told me."

She stepped away from the door and worry etched little creases around her sad eyes. "Are you sure? Because I'm a mess and I hate to drag you into my problems. You should probably run in the other direction."

He smiled at her. "Hey. A kid who's growing up and pulling away…sounds vaguely familiar."

She breathed deeply and laughed. A real laugh, as if the tension had gone out of her. "Yeah, I'll try to think positively." She opened the door to the café. "You know, I just want our visit this summer to be perfect. I want to recapture the relationship we had before he changed. Before he went to live with his dad. I just want my little boy again."

Gabe swallowed, because he totally understood that pain. That longing. "I hope you get that, Faith. I really do."

"Thank you."

He inhaled slowly and steeled his nerves. "Your hair looks nice, by the way."

Her hand flew up to brush the hair back from her face—a face now streaked with red. "Does it? I don't know if I like it."

He touched the ends of it, then snatched his traitorous hand away. "Yeah. Very nice." And soft and silky and smelling fine.

"Thanks." She bolted inside and darted behind the counter.

Lord…Faith and Ben really need Your help right

now. I ask that You be with them, help them work out their relationship.

A better man would have remained faithful to God through the bad times. Gabe hoped God would forgive him for straying, would listen to his prayer.

He stuck his head inside. "Chels, I'll be back later to pick you up."

She barely waved, the child who looked so much like him.

And even after all the upset that fact had caused not ten minutes ago, he now found that it made him just the tiniest bit happy. Maybe with God's help he could grow to embrace change after all.

On Sunday morning, Faith tried desperately to dry her hair like the stylist had done the day before. But with no luck whatsoever. And she was running late. Audra and Gary had asked her to drive Chelsea that morning.

So she tried to put her hair in her standard ponytail, but the layers started to slip out. "Oh, forget it."

She tossed the rubber band into a drawer and ran a brush through the resistant strands. Though her hair wouldn't cooperate, she took time to put on some makeup, then decided to walk next door to get Chelsea rather than honk the horn from the driveway.

Why am I going to this trouble? Because he said he liked my new haircut?

She refused to believe she was doing it for a chance to see Gabe. No way. She was merely being neighborly.

Great. Now she was defending her actions…to herself. A total clue she needed to get a grip on her feelings.

She could not be interested in a man who'd be looking for a good mother for his child. A man who was still in love with his dead wife—a man who had a fit because his daughter didn't look like the woman anymore. It would be reckless. And lead to nothing but pain.

As she rang the doorbell, her treacherous heart raced. She mashed a hand to her chest, wishing she could force her heart into submission.

Gabe opened the door dressed in a black suit and red-striped tie, wearing a tense smile.

Her heart kerplunked to about the level of her stomach. Then it kicked back into high gear. "Wow. Something special going on at work today?"

His smiled collapsed. "No, I'm actually going to church."

"Oh. Wow." *Okay, Faith. Say something that makes sense.* "Um, I'm glad. I guess Chelsea won't need a ride, after all."

"No. In fact, I'm going to be taking Sundays off like I used to. And I've agreed to help Phil by working with the youth on Sunday nights."

Triple wow. "That's fantastic. I'm sure Chelsea is thrilled."

"She's pretty happy. She's been begging me to attend services with her each week."

"I'm sure the kids will love you." And Phil wanted her to help the youth, too? How could God expect her to work with Gabe each week with the way she'd been feeling?

"I'm ready," Chelsea called as she walked into the room behind Gabe. "Oh, hi, Faith. Are you riding with us?"

"Um, no," Gabe said. "We just forgot to tell Audra and Gary that you didn't need a ride."

Lovely. He didn't want her riding with them any more than she wanted to. "That's okay. I'm glad your dad will be taking you now." She waved to the two of them. "See you there."

"Well, that's just crazy," Chelsea said. "You should ride with us." She wormed her way beside her dad and through the screen door. Then as if she knew Faith was about to run, she hooked her arm through Faith's. "Come on, Dad. Let's go."

Faith didn't want to look at him. She really didn't. But her eyes were drawn to him anyway.

He smiled at her and shrugged. "Then let's go."

A few minutes later, they drove up to the redbrick church, its white steeple gleaming in the morning sun as if happy to see them.

When they arrived at the church sanctuary, Faith was hit with the dilemma of what to do. Sit with them or in her regular pew?

As folks around them gaped or grinned, she

debated about whether the stares were over Gabe showing up or over the fact that the three of them had come in together. Whatever the cause of the commotion, she made an easy decision. She would flee to her own little spot.

"Thanks for the ride," she whispered.

Before she could get away, Chelsea grabbed her hand. And held firm. "Sit with us," she ordered.

"Um..."

"Please?"

She glanced over Chelsea's head. Gabe looked as if his tie was strangling him. He forced a smile that probably hurt. "Yes, please join us."

The look on his face was almost comical. But Chelsea's wasn't. She was earnest in her invitation. So Faith accepted and followed them to the opposite side of the aisle, about three quarters of the way to the front.

Where lots of people could watch them.

Oh, brother. There was nothing worse than being on display. Though she needed to get over it. They were merely neighbors sharing a ride. And a pew.

But the knot in her stomach said otherwise. The situation with Gabe and Chelsea *had* become more to her than that. It felt nice to have Gabe drive her that morning. Felt nice to have someone to walk into church with. Felt nice to have someone invite her to sit with them.

Scary nice.

She was pathetic. And lonely. And she was thankful that Ben would be there soon to help fill her time so she wouldn't have this outrageous yearning to be part of something she couldn't have—Gabe's family.

Gabe couldn't have felt more conspicuous if he'd staggered down the aisle of the sanctuary drunk. Thanks to Chelsea—and Faith—there wasn't a shred of hope of gradually easing back into attending worship services.

Once they took their seats, he looked beside him at Chelsea…and Faith. If he'd thought an empty spot in the church pew was bad, then this was worse: having someone else sitting in Tina's place.

No matter how good and kind and helpful Faith was, seeing her sitting beside his daughter where Tina should have been was, well, uncomfortable at best.

He couldn't even focus on the message. Or the music. Or anything else for that matter.

He kept looking to his side expecting to find the two women in his life with their long, dark brown curls. And now he found one girl with her short, wild hair. And one woman with layers of light golden brown.

Nothing felt right.

He tried to recall Tina's face and the feel of her kiss, but Faith's seafoam eyes and full, inviting lips flashed into his mind and wouldn't budge. The image was so startlingly real, he jerked to look at Faith.

And caught her staring back. She smiled shyly before glancing away.

When Faith put her arm around Chelsea to whisper something, and her fingers brushed his shoulder, he nearly sprang out of his seat.

Guilt, raw and biting, locked him into facing forward. How could he think about Faith's lips when his beloved wife was gone?

He should be focusing on his daughter. Needed to pull himself together. That guilt was there for a reason. To convict him. He shouldn't be thinking of himself and his needs when Chelsea was struggling.

But she's not struggling now that Faith is in the picture.

He snapped open the hymn book and belted out the last song, trying to drown out thoughts of Faith.

He could hardly wait to escape. He wanted to toss his keys to Faith and then walk home. But good manners dictated he act civil on the way out of the church building.

"Oh, Gabe, honey, I'm so happy you've finally found a girlfriend," said Lilly, one of the matriarchs of the church, as she patted his arm. "And she's such a peach. Of course, I've been praying for you to find the perfect match." She smiled, then gripped her cane tighter and tottered away.

Chelsea made a peeping sound. She slapped a hand over her mouth to keep from laughing.

He glared at Faith.

Her face glowed scarlet. "I promise I had nothing to do with Miss Lilly's prayers."

But Faith and Chelsea had started the whole matchmaking mess. He plowed ahead, through the doors of the church, then to the bottom of the steps where the pastor greeted everyone. He couldn't very well blow past him, so he waited his turn, hoping to get out of there as soon as possible.

Phil's eyes lit up as he grabbed Gabe's hand and pumped it. "I sure am glad to see you here this morning. And you'll be here tonight?"

"Of course."

"Oh, there you are, Chief Reynolds," said Mrs. Hunt with her blond-streaked hair. She hooked her arm through his and steered him away from the pastor. "Did you get a chance to call my Kelli Lyn yet?"

"Um, no ma'am. You see, I'm not dating."

"That's not what I hear," said another woman from behind him. Hazel. Apparently, she'd sneaked up on them. She leaned toward Mrs. Hunt. "It looks like that Faith Hagin has caught his eye."

"Uh, no, ladies. You have this all wrong."

"Come on, Chief. Don't be embarrassed. I understand a man needs a good woman by his side.

Especially with a child to think of." Hazel leaned closer. "I have a great-niece you might be interested in, though. She's about your age. Never been married." She raised a brow at Mrs. Hunt, then she slipped a piece of paper into his jacket pocket and patted it. "Call her."

He'd had all he could take. He turned to escape and ran smack-dab into Faith. He gripped her arms to keep from knocking her down. "Oh, excuse me."

They both stood frozen. Her arms were cool from the air-conditioned building. The skin was so smooth. He looked into her eyes and—

"Uh-huh." Hazel tugged on the lapels of her red polyester blazer. "What'd I tell you?"

He had to get out of there.

He stalked toward the car while calling over his shoulder, "Time to go." He didn't look back. Just assumed they were following.

This dating thing was even more out of hand than he'd imagined. He didn't know what he could do, short of making some sort of announcement at a church service.

I have a newsflash for all of you. I'm not looking for a date, so leave me alone. I still love my wife and have no plans to love again.

Yeah, he could just imagine how well that would go over. Not his idea of a fun Sunday at church.

Of course, it couldn't be much worse than today.

At least that evening he could count on spending time with his daughter and her friends at the youth meeting. No matchmaking ladies from the church.

And more importantly, no Faith Hagin.

Chapter Seven

Okay. Wake-up call. Faith had to get her mind off Gabe and back on her own plans.

Determined to forge ahead with her already complicated-enough life, Faith went online to buy baseball tickets for Ben's visit. She thought it would be fun to go to an Atlanta Braves game together. The Braves would be playing the Giants that week—and Ben's favorite baseball player was with the Giants now.

Thrilled to find fantastic seats on one of the ticket-swap sites, she quickly purchased the tickets.

The night together at the game would be perfect.

She grinned as she dialed his cell phone, knowing how happy he'd be to hear the news.

"Hey, Mom." His Eeyore tone of voice spoke volumes.

"Hi, sweetie. How'd the tournament go?"

"We're still in it."

"Oh, really? That's great. When do you play again?"

"Tomorrow evening in the finals."

"How exciting. You'll have to call and let me know how it goes."

"I'll try, if it's not too late. Plus, we have to leave at five the next morning. Have two doubleheaders back in Georgia later in the week."

"Just keep in touch. And, hey, I wanted you to know I have some fun things planned for your visit." Her grin widened and her pulse raced. "You won't believe what I got. Tenth-row seats right behind home plate for the Braves versus Giants."

Silence greeted the wonderful news.

"Ben?"

"I just wish you'd wait until this tournament is over before making any more plans."

"Why? What happens if you win?"

He sighed. "There's no way we'll win. The team we have to play tomorrow killed us last time we played them. There's no chance."

A sick fist gripped her stomach. "But what if you do beat them?"

"Look, I've gotta go. Dad's at the door."

"Okay, honey. Have a safe trip."

They hung up and she had to fight tears. Because she just knew that his team was probably going to do the impossible and beat the top team and end up in another tournament the week he was supposed to arrive.

Lord, You know how badly Ben and I need uninterrupted time together. Help us to work this out.

And I pray for the healing of our relationship no matter the outcome of the game.

Well, it was in God's hands now, but she still had to do her part. She had to hire and train someone—hopefully Juanita Alvarez—to help Natalie while Ben was here. First thing Monday morning, she'd give Juanita a call.

In the meantime, she headed to the café to do the best she could on her own. Sunday evenings were usually one of her busiest times, but she'd committed to transporting kids to and from the youth meeting again this week. She had to briefly close the shop twice to do so.

Only this time, she didn't need to transport Chelsea. Gabe would be volunteering.

She managed one trip to the church without running into Gabe. Later that evening, when she arrived to take the kids back home, she found Gabe in the parking lot throwing a football with a group of boys and girls—Chelsea among them.

As she waited for her riders, Gabe motioned to her to hold up. He tossed the football to Chelsea and approached.

She put the window down and tried not to drown in the humidity that smacked her in the face. "Did you need something?"

"Uh, yeah. Phil told me he'd asked you to help on Sunday nights." He inclined his head to the youth outside. "He wanted me to ask you if you'd be willing to be my assistant."

Great. Now someone else knew Phil had asked her. “Tell him I’m sorry, but I just don’t have the time right now, even to be an assistant.”

Relief washed over Gabe’s face.

Which sent a burst of anger sparking through her like a hot poker. “You don’t have to look so happy about it.”

She snapped her mouth shut, mortified.

His eyes widened, but then the surprise turned to humor. He gave a short laugh. Then he leaned close to her ear. “Sorry. It’s just that after today at church, I’m not sure we should be hanging out together. People will get the wrong idea.”

And how terrible for them to think you might care about me.

The comment stung, even though she wished it hadn’t. Even though she wished she could feel the same way.

But no. She’d had to go and start caring what he thought of her.

Had started caring, period.

She waved over her riders and they climbed in. She began to roll up the window. “I’ve gotta go. I still need to close up the café for the night.” She drove away before he could say anything else that might hurt her feelings. She didn’t think she could take one more disappointment that day or she might break down and cry.

Faith swallowed back the hurt and put on a smile for the three youths she was delivering back to their homes. Once she'd dropped them off, she forced herself to think of something besides Gabe.

Ben. She could focus on his visit.

When she reached the café, she parked in the back and walked into the kitchen. Maybe she'd get online and do some research on renting a boat at the lake. Ben had always enjoyed swimming. She could ask him to bring his water skis. They could have a picnic and spend a day on the water. And then—

Something rattled in her office.

She stopped in her tracks. She couldn't see inside her office, so she stood still and waited. And then she heard the rattle again. She started to call out, but something made her stop short. *The back door.* Had it been locked when she came in? She hadn't even noticed. And since she'd only closed up briefly, she hadn't set the alarm.

She inched away from her office toward the back door, then noticed the door to the supply closet was open.

She never left that closet open. Someone had been looking for something.

The desk chair creaked, just like it did if she sat down.

Or got up.

A chill shot through her body, making her dizzy. She bit her lip to keep from screaming. Someone was coming. She darted into the supply closet.

After squeezing through the door, trying not to bump the mop bucket, she slowly pulled the closet door closed, grateful that the hinges didn't squeak like the other doors in the building.

A loud bang sounded in her office, accompanied by a man's cursing. He was probably trying to get in the safe.

With her heart threatening to burst out of her throat, she fumbled for her cell phone.

Lord, please let Gabe answer.

It had been tough for Gabe to take a whole day off. Though Fred was very capable, he hadn't been on the job long. So that night after Gabe and Chelsea finished up at the church, they stopped by the station to check in.

"You can't get away from your job, can you?" Chelsea asked as they walked inside.

"I just want to check on Fred."

"And make sure he did everything the way you'd do it?" She laughed at him. "You can't stand not being in control, can you?"

He tried to give her a censuring look, but he ended up smiling. After he greeted Fred, his young, energetic—and a tad cocky—deputy, he said hello to the dispatcher, Wanda. Wanda, with her dark gray hair and grandmotherly demeanor, stole Fred's thunder by giving a report on all the calls that day. Pretty quiet, overall.

"Sounds like you two have everything under control," Gabe said. "I'll see you in the morning."

As they were heading toward the door, his cell phone rang. “Reynolds,” he answered.

“Gabe?” Faith whispered. “Someone’s broken into the café. I walked in on him.”

Adrenaline shot through his veins, making his body nearly buzz. “Are you somewhere safe?”

“I’m in the supply closet.”

“I’m on my way.”

“Please hurry,” she said on a breath, so quietly he could hardly hear her.

“I will. Stay on the line with me.” He turned Chelsea around and pointed to the dispatch desk. “Stay here with Wanda. Fred, let’s get over to the coffee shop. Faith walked in on a break-in.”

Fred bolted out of his chair. “Let’s go.”

“Dad?” Tears welled in Chelsea’s eyes.

“She’ll be okay.” He would see to it.

Lord, keep her safe.

They ran out to Fred’s car. Gabe gritted his teeth in frustration. He couldn’t slow his pounding heart. Usually, he was cool in these situations. All business. But for some reason, this one had him…

Scared.

No, he couldn’t be.

But he was scared. Because the victim was Faith.

As Fred drove to the back entrance of the café, Gabe punched his foot to the floorboard, trying to make Fred go faster. “You still okay?” he asked into the phone.

“Yes. He’s in my office messing with the safe.”

"That's good. Just stay put."

She huffed a quiet laugh. "Oh, don't worry."

Don't worry? Yeah, right.

Just when Gabe thought his chest would explode, they finally approached the back door. "Faith, honey, we're here. Hang on." He disconnected as he checked the area.

No vehicles besides Faith's. The intruder was on foot. Or had someone waiting nearby.

Grateful he'd rearmed himself after leaving the church, he took out his gun. He and Fred quietly inspected the lock, which was broken, and entered the kitchen. Noise sounded from Faith's office. He motioned to Fred to cover him. Then Fred leaned around the door frame to ascertain the situation.

Gabe found the guy trying to pry the safe open with a screwdriver. "Okay, buddy, game's over. Put your hands on top of your head."

Within seconds, they had the unarmed man cuffed and the café secured.

As Fred handled the perpetrator, Gabe hurried to what appeared to be the supply closet. "Faith, it's me. Come on out."

"Thank you, Lord," she said in a muffled voice. The door flew open. In a blur of motion, she ran out, threw her arms around his neck and held tight. "I've never been so glad to see someone in my life."

He grinned and wrapped his arms around her waist. Couldn't help himself. He closed his eyes. Breathed in. He didn't want to let go. And not just because he was relieved she was safe. No, he realized this had just as much to do with enjoying the fact she was clinging to him.

Her heart pounded against his chest. "All I could think about were ax murderers."

"Thankfully, he was only after the money in your safe," he said, still unwilling to let her out of his arms. Even when he knew he should lecture her on being more observant for signs of forced entry.

"It would've been empty. I visited the night deposit box on the way to the church." She leaned far enough away to look him in the eye and they both laughed.

Her blue eyes, dotted with flecks of green, darted to his lips. "I'm so glad you answered your phone."

That made him do what he should have done sooner. He set her away from him. But he didn't totally release her until he'd rubbed his hands over her shoulders and down her arms to assure she was in one piece. He looked her over.

She looked just fine.

Too fine.

He forced a stern frown on his face to replace the idiotic smile he'd been sporting. "You should never dial my cell phone in an emergency, Faith. You should have dialed 911."

"Well, you're here, so that's what matters."

"I just happened to be at the station when you called. If I'd been at the church, it would have wasted precious time. The guy wouldn't have been happy to find an empty safe. He may have found you instead."

She appeared properly chastised. "I never thought of that. I just thought…well…of you." As soon as she said it, a blush stole up along her cheekbones, making her even more beautiful.

Oh, man. He needed his protective equipment right now. To protect him from the crazy thrill her statement gave him. "Why don't you go check for property damage."

"Sure." She hurried into motion as if glad to escape their closeness.

With the distance, he could finally breathe deeply again. He followed her around the café, and it appeared the perp's only target was the safe.

Fred stuck his head in the back door. "I'm heading to the county jail. You want a ride to the station?"

"Be right there."

"So you need to go, too, I guess," Faith said, almost as if she wanted him to stay. Of course, she must still be frightened.

But at the moment, he needed some space. To see if he could figure out what had just happened between them. "Chels is waiting at the station with Wanda. I'll send Wanda over to stay with you while you close up."

"Thanks." She gave him a crooked smile. Could it be that she even looked disappointed?

He clenched his fists. No way was he even allowing that train of thought to take root. "Don't forget. Dial 911 if you have an emergency. Always set the alarms. And for goodness' sake, if the door lock ever looks jimmied, don't enter."

"Normally, I wouldn't. I guess I was just distracted." She grabbed a broom and held it in front her like a protective barrier. "I need to clean up for the night."

He couldn't get out of there fast enough. Couldn't get far enough away from his pretty neighbor. She'd totally scrambled his brains. "Well, be more careful next time."

"I will, Chief."

Yes. *Chief* was good. Back to a professional relationship. No more calling him, scaring the life out of him…hugging him.

Lord, You know how difficult the past few years have been. And now I'm struggling—liking the feel of a woman in my arms a little too much. Help me stay strong.

Yes, he would need God's help. Because if he found Faith in his arms again, he wasn't sure he'd be able to resist the temptation to keep her there.

Faith's eyes flew open before the alarm clock went off on Monday morning. *Ben's tournament final is today.*

Down the hall sat an empty bedroom, decorated in dark blue with shelves holding some of Ben's first baseball trophies. Would he ever spend the night there?

She blinked away sleepiness as she peered around her neat-as-a-pin bedroom in the early morning light. The room looked barely lived in since she spent most of her time at the shop.

The shop. Memories of the break-in rushed in. Memories of Gabe, as well.

Ben… Gabe… Ben's game… Hugging Gabe…

She snapped her attention back to the problem. How to handle her feelings for Gabe. If she couldn't resolve her relationship with Ben—which she feared was a real possibility—would Gabe ever fully trust her with his daughter?

She climbed out of bed to spend some time in prayer before heading to work. Tried to center herself, asking God to fill her with peace.

But when she arrived at the café, she found her self-appointed protectors sitting outside the back door in the squad car, and her calm attitude flew right out the window.

Gabe and Chelsea.

Gabe. She'd thrown herself into his arms last night.

And, oh, my. He was as strong and solid as he looked.

Remembering the feel of his arms wrapped around her, she pressed her hand against her chest, trying to contain the ache for more.

Now he was being overly protective by showing up at the café first thing. She steeled herself for seeing him in uniform, freshly out of the shower with wet hair. Smelling like soap mixed with man. But not just any man. His scent was even more intoxicating.

"You need to get this lock repaired today," he said as soon as he stepped out of the car.

She really had to figure a way to help with Chelsea, yet keep Gabe at arm's length.

She joined her two friends by the back door of the shop. "Good morning. No need to patrol so early. I'll be safe."

Chelsea inspected the damaged door. "Were you scared?"

Gabe stared at Faith, yet he wasn't smiling like usual. He seemed aloof. And all business.

Good. "Yes. I was terrified. But your dad and Fred caught the guy." She sorted through her key ring. "Thanks for meeting me this morning, you two. But I'm fine." She bobbled the key as she tried to put it in the barely latched lock.

Gabe reached around her.

She sucked in a quick breath as his arm slid along her arm, the hairs on his brushing the sensitive skin of hers.

"Here." He snatched the key, opened the door and motioned for her to enter. The security system beeped. "Can you manage the alarm code?"

"Of course," she snapped, praying her hands would quit shaking so she could do it within the forty-five second delay. If the man would just move farther away she'd function so much better.

She jabbed at the numbers on the alarm panel. It took two tries, but she turned it off without assistance.

Being all business was one thing. But why did he

act so angry? When he didn't show signs of leaving quickly enough to suit Faith, she said, "Chelsea, how about helping me bake cinnamon sticky buns?"

"I'd love to. Bye, Dad." She reached up to hug his neck.

He looked at Faith over Chelsea's head. Then he kissed his daughter and left.

Faith made the quickest about-face ever and grabbed her apron. "Time to start baking."

Chelsea didn't budge. She ran her finger up and down the door frame. "It's pretty cool that Dad rescued you."

Faith froze in the middle of tying the apron strings. "And Fred, too."

"Yeah, well, I was thinking maybe this is what we've been praying for."

Faith's heart sank. When Chelsea looked up, Faith could see the hope in her eyes. *Please don't let her get hurt.* "No, we've been praying for the perfect woman to come along. And I don't fit that bill."

Chelsea shrugged. "Maybe God thinks you do."

Faith's fingers shook as she tried to smile. She needed to tread carefully. "Sweetie, your dad and I are friends. I honestly think he still loves your mom." She rubbed Chelsea's back, hoping to reassure her even as she dealt with her own doubt. "Be patient with him. Someday, the right woman will come along."

Most men would learn to love again. But not Gabe. Because no one would ever measure up to Tina.

And Faith better remember that the next time he came riding up on a white horse.

Chapter Eight

By Monday evening, Gabe found himself buried alive under what, for him, was a mountain of paperwork. Lately, he'd tried hard to be home more with Chelsea, so now he needed to file accident reports, court dockets and deposit tickets. He also had an equipment maintenance file to update.

For the first time ever, stacks of file folders covered most of his desk. Yet, the most stressful part of his day had been the request from Chelsea to go to a movie with Valerie and her parents. The fact that he was swamped and would be late for dinner swayed his decision.

After speaking with Olivia and being assured the adults wouldn't let the girls out of their sight, he gave his permission for her to go.

Once he made a good dent in the mound on his desk, he headed home. Faith would be watching Chelsea during the evening three days that week. And her car was still in his driveway.

His mind flashed to Faith's arms around his neck, her silky hair tickling his cheek, her warm breath on his neck as she thanked him.

His protective vest felt like it contracted as he tried to breathe normally and gain control of his thoughts.

This woman was simply his neighbor, he reminded himself. The woman who'd been helping with Chelsea.

The woman he'd grown to count on to care for his child.

The woman who smelled like flowers and sweetness and something fresh. With beautiful aqua eyes. With a sweet heart-shaped face.

When he realized he was sitting in the car with the engine cut off, and the temperature rising by the second, he forced his feet to move. He could deal with her in his home. Besides, maybe she'd gone home but hadn't bothered to move her car.

As he was about to reach for the front doorknob, the door opened.

"Oh, hi, Gabe. I was just leaving."

"So Chels left?"

"About five minutes ago. Your dinner's on a plate in the oven."

A very wifely thing to do, and definitely not part of their babysitting arrangement. Why was he so disappointed she was leaving when he should be relieved? "Thanks. Uh, did you eat already?"

"Sort of."

"Sort of?" He laughed, took her elbow to lead her back into the house and shut the door behind them. "Then come on back and eat with me."

He didn't take the time to think about what he was doing. He led her to the kitchen—which was spotless since Faith had been there. Every surface gleamed. He held a chair out for her at the table, then said, "So what did you eat?"

"A roll."

"That's it?" He pulled the plate out of the oven, nearly burning himself in the process. It landed with a thud on the countertop. He removed the foil and found chicken nuggets, mashed potatoes and green beans. "You've given me enough for an army."

"Honestly, I should go. I left Juanita for a couple of hours on her first day."

He grinned. "So she took the job. Good." He was glad he'd called and talked to her. She seemed reassured after their conversation. "Come on, you've got to eat."

Faith assented, so he grabbed an extra plate and split the food. Then he poured two glasses of iced tea and sat down across the table from her. Overwhelmed with sudden gratitude for Faith and all she'd done for him—as well as for how God had patiently watched over them for the last few years, he held out a hand, inviting Faith to pray with him.

She stared at his outstretched hand.

"Let's bless the food." A habit he'd let slip for quite a while.

"Oh, okay." She quickly placed her hand in his as she bowed her head.

"Dear Lord, thank You for this food and bless it to the nourishment of our bodies and us to Thy service." It was the rote prayer he'd said for most of his adult life but hadn't said since his wife's death. And at the moment, he wanted to say so much more. *Thank You for this warm, loving hand that prepared my meal. Thank You that she takes good care of Chelsea so I can work where You've called me to work. Thank You that she's helping me want to talk to You again.* "Amen."

He raised his head but didn't let go of her hand.

She was staring at him. "Amen," she added, as if she'd been waiting for him to finish his silent prayer. Then she curled her fingers and slid her soft hand out of his.

He put his napkin in his lap. "This looks so good. Thank you for feeding Chels. And for making this for me."

"I'm happy to do it. Chelsea said she was craving chicken nuggets, so we ran to the store for ingredients and I taught her how to make them." She picked at her food. Barely eating. Had she been as bothered by their contact the day before as he had?

And now she was teaching Chels to cook? He owed her so much. "I really appreciate it. There's so much a woman could teach her that she's missing out on."

"I realize that. But she'll be fine. You're a good dad. She feels loved, even if she does get frustrated."

"Yeah, maybe so. It's more than I got from my parents."

She glanced up and raised her brows in question.

He wasn't going into details, but it couldn't hurt to share a little about himself. "My mother basically deserted our family. Suffice it to say I decided to do better for myself and my children. I picked a wife who would be a good mom."

"I'm sorry about your mom." She stared at her potatoes. "From what I've heard, you couldn't have picked better than Tina."

He nodded as he ate another mouthful, surprised he could talk about it at all. "You know, in the beginning, I worried that I married her more for the mother she could be than for love."

Faith swallowed. Took a long drink of her tea. Then looked at her plate. "So did you love her?"

"Of course. It was just a crazy notion. Probably out of fear of making that big commitment. I wasn't sure I'd be good at marriage."

"Well, apparently you were. I've heard the two of you were very happy."

He stared at the table—which Tina had bought. At the walls she had painted. "Yes, I miss her. Everywhere I look, something reminds me of her."

"Have you thought about making some changes?" She winced as if sorry to have mentioned something painful, then quickly shook her head. "You know. Just something little. To help move ahead."

But that was the problem. He didn't want to move ahead. He wanted to keep the memories alive. "Chelsea wants new living-room furniture, something less formal, more comfortable. But I just can't let the old stuff go. Tina bought it." He smiled at the memory. "She bought a new sofa because she hated our old worn-out one. When I got home from work one day, my beloved plaid man-couch from my bachelor days sat at the curb."

Faith smiled up at him. Then she burst into laughter. "I can just see you out there by the road grieving."

He chuckled, too. "Yeah, Chels and I had a memorial service for it before the garbage collectors hauled it off."

She reached across the table and laid her hand over his. "It might help with Chelsea if she sees you moving forward. I think the two of you buying a nice, comfy sectional would be a good place to start."

To start what? he wanted to ask.

But he knew she was right. They did need to move on with their lives. He just wasn't ready.

"I appreciate that you're trying to help." He brushed her knuckles with his thumb and watched a blush steal up her neck and face.

He could make her blush. And he liked that about her.

“You can tell me to butt out if you want,” she said. “It won’t hurt my feelings.”

“Okay. Butt out.” He smiled at her, because for some reason it was important to see her smile back. To have her look him in the eye.

She seemed shocked at his statement, but then once she read his expression, she grinned. “Okay. I’ll try.”

“Good.” He realized their hands were still touching and pulled his away.

“You know, more than a new couch, your daughter wants you to start dating. And I think Hannah would be a good match for you and Chelsea.”

“I deduced that.” He smirked.

She ignored him and held up a finger. “She’s a widow so she would understand where you’re coming from.” A second finger popped up. “And she’s such a great mom. And, as a bonus, she’s beautiful.”

Yes, but he couldn’t drum up one bit of attraction to the woman. He shrugged. “I’m sorry I can’t make Chelsea happy in that area. Interest in another woman would feel like betraying Tina.”

Faith carried her plate to the sink and turned away from him. “Oh, I know. I’m sorry.”

He hopped up and stepped behind her. He put his hands on the counter on either side of her to stop her scurrying to clean up. “Do you understand, really?

Hemmed in by his arms, she stilled, turned and looked into his eyes. And he could see the talk of Tina had hurt her.

He sucked in a breath. *Oh, no.* She couldn't care for him. It was crazy. Beyond crazy. "I still love my wife. I'm not going to date. Don't even want to."

She lifted one of his arms out of her way and moved to the table. "I totally understand. I'm sure I'd feel the same."

He just hoped she truly did. Because he couldn't allow himself to really *care* about any woman.

If he did, he might lose her, too.

On Tuesday, as Faith opened the Coffee Time Café doors to a lined-up breakfast crowd, she greeted each by name and tried her best to appear as if Natalie hadn't just knocked her for a loop by walking in for work with a wedding band on her finger. Faith's best employee had come in early, tears in her eyes, yet glowing with happiness. They'd discussed the shocking news, and Faith had given her blessing.

She eloped. She's married. And is moving to Tennessee. With her head still spinning, Faith put up a good front and made coffee on autopilot.

Just one foot in front of the other. Somehow, she would make it through the day.

About the time the line died down and the café began to empty of customers, the door opened again. *Gabe.*

Tears that had threatened all morning nearly spilled over at the sight of him.

She squeezed her eyes shut and busied herself

cleaning the back of the pastry display case. What if she broke down in front of him?

Gabe approached the counter. “Good morning.”

She sprayed the glass a second time and attacked it with a paper towel. “I’ll be right with you.” *Hold it together, Faith.*

“I just need my doughnut fix for today.”

Out of the corner of her eye, she saw that he smiled. Was teasing her. Probably to ease the awkwardness from last night at his house.

She didn’t trust her voice, so she simply nodded.

With a light touch, he laid his hand on her shoulder. “Is everything okay?”

She flinched away from his care. “Yes. Fine.” She slapped the bottle of cleaner on the counter, smoothed her apron and then made herself look right at him. “Would you like your regular?”

His concerned expression made tears burn her eyes.

He walked around the end of the counter and didn’t stop until he was a foot away and right in her face. “I’m sorry if I said something yesterday that offended you.”

“Oh, it’s not that.” She took in a jerky breath as she glanced into the kitchen. “Natalie had gone home to announce her engagement and ended up eloping. She’s moving in a week.”

Tension in his stance eased. “I’m sorry. I know you’ve been counting on her to take over while you’re on vacation.”

"Yeah. But, I have Juanita and I've lined up two interviews for this afternoon. I'm hopeful." She tried to look brave, but she suspected he could see right through it.

He took a step closer so that they were pretty much toe-to-toe. "It'll work out."

"I must sound selfish," she whispered. "I'm not only concerned for my vacation. My first thought was for Natalie, because I followed my new husband, too—and got ditched for parties and college life. But that's crazy, because Vince is a good guy."

He flinched and she wished she hadn't been so blunt about her past.

"It's not just any vacation," he said. "You're worried about your relationship with Ben."

"I still haven't been able to reach him about the outcome of the game, so I assume he's still coming." She tilted her head back. Swallowed. "I need this time with Ben so badly."

"I know."

"He's all grown-up. And…and…" She snapped her fingers. "…poof, he'll be gone off to college. And I can't bear if he leaves and is still angry with me."

He pushed her bangs back from her forehead. "Angry about what?"

His gentle touch…his caring… It made her want to talk, to share her pain. "Nothing. Everything. I don't really know."

"I'll do anything I can to help with Ben. Or around here. Let me know what you need, okay?"

"Thanks, Gabe." She wanted to lay her head on his shoulder, to let him reassure her.

But he moved away. "Then I guess this isn't a good day for Chels to hang out."

They were back to neighborly chat about his daughter. "No, I'm sorry."

"No problem. I just promised her I'd ask on my way to work."

She jerked up straight and smoothed her already smooth apron. So he hadn't come by to see *her.* "And here I am, acting like a big baby and keeping you waiting for your doughnuts." She turned quickly and reached for the tongs.

Something tugged on the bow at the waist of her apron and stopped her motion. When she turned, Gabe wrapped her in a hug. "You're not a big baby. You're stronger and more giving than any woman I know."

Faith froze. She wanted to bolt. One minute he pulled away and talked about Chelsea, but the next, he was hugging her, whispering comfort?

She stiffened but almost immediately melted into his arms. How could she not? It seemed he was trying to be a good friend. Supportive. Kind.

Strong. Solid.

And he smelled so good she wanted to burrow into his uniform shirt. She managed not to burrow, but she inhaled deeply. Then she let her stress ease out on a big sigh.

She also slipped her arms around his waist.

And now she really did want to cry. Because she could get so used to this.

Only Gabe wasn't hers for the taking. He belonged to Tina.

Tina Forever. She could imagine it as a billboard hanging around his neck.

Someone cleared her throat behind them.

Gabe jerked away, leaving Faith bereft. And a little senseless. She nearly yanked him back.

But Miss Ann stood on the other side of the counter grinning. "Hello, you two."

Faith's face raged hot and mortified.

Gabe looked as if he'd choked down a dozen doughnut holes in one bite. "Hello, Miss Ann."

"Carry on. I can come back later."

"No!"

"No." Gabe said at the same instant.

Faith pointed to the dining room. "Have a seat. I'll bring your hot chocolate right out. Gabe and I were just—"

"Hugging," he finished for her. As if it weren't obvious. "Just a friendly hug between neighbors."

Faith nearly groaned. At least she'd shut her mouth before making it worse.

Ann's eyes sparkled, and Faith could imagine her licking her chops, dying to run out and advertise the embrace she'd just witnessed. "No need to explain. I'll just run to the drugstore."

"No, ma'am. I was leaving. I'm late for my shift." Gabe didn't look at either of them as he stalked out the door of the café. Without his doughnuts.

Merely watching him walk away sent Faith's pulse into overdrive. She did moan this time. Out loud. In agony. "Oh, Ann. I'm so in over my head."

Ann clapped her hands together. "And I'm so excited to see this."

"You don't want to get excited over this. It's nothing. Has to be nothing."

"Oh, I saw more than 'nothing,' dear."

Faith pulled out a chair and plopped down. "What you saw was a big mistake. He felt sorry for me and tried to make it better." She watched as his car pulled away from the curb. "And he didn't even get his breakfast."

"Why would he feel sorry for you? You're smart, beautiful, successful..."

"Natalie gave her notice today. He knew how difficult it'll be for me to take my vacation now." *And he understands. And he offered to help.*

Ann sat beside her and patted her shoulder. "I'm sorry, dear. But maybe this is a blessing in disguise. It might bring you two closer."

But closer was not a good thing anymore. He loved Tina. And even if he was miraculously able to move on, Faith would never be good enough in his eyes to mother Chelsea. Especially if he ever found out the whole story about Ben.

Why did the one man she thought she could actually trust have to be so out of reach?

Chapter Nine

The next evening, Gabe pulled up at the station in a foul mood. Another headache meeting with the mayor, who wanted Gabe to somehow expand services with a shrinking budget.

But at least Chelsea had been able to spend the day with Faith and not have to hang out and watch Kristy study. He didn't have to add parental guilt to the frustrations of the day.

His cell phone rang.

Faith.

Now, why did that fact have to send a thrill raging through his body? He snatched the phone open. "Hello, Faith."

"It's dinnertime." Her bright, cheery voice put a dent in his bad temper.

He almost smiled. "And…?"

"And you have a split shift, so you get to eat with your daughter at the covered-dish dinner at church tonight."

Chelsea yelled something in the background.

Faith added, "Chelsea invited me to come along, if you don't mind."

The frustrations of the day slipped away. "Sure. I'd—*we'd* love that. I planned to buy a bucket of fried chicken."

"No worries. I've made enough pot roast and potato salad for all of us."

"She has," his daughter yelled into the phone. "Dessert, too! Come pick us up at Faith's house."

The fact that his daughter was having fun and was happy helped drain the last of the tension out of his shoulders. He needed to keep reminding himself what was most important.

Family.

But should family time include Faith?

The thought nagged at him all the way to her house. As soon as he drove up and found Faith and Chelsea outside, arms loaded with dishes of food, laughing, a sense of rightness calmed him.

Yes. Including Faith. Chelsea was obviously happier.

But could he do that? Could he truly move on with his life and try to include someone else in their family?

He hopped out of the squad car to help put the food in the trunk. Faith's perfume wafted his way. Her arm brushed against his as she rearranged the pans he'd placed, making them more secure.

When she looked him in the eye and smiled, then dusted her hands off and said, "There. Thanks for helping," his heart told him that yes, he could at least try to include her. Maybe even pursue some sort of…relationship. Because surely it wouldn't be a hardship.

"Anytime," he said. He smiled back at her, his heart thudding in his chest like some love-struck teenager.

But once they were in the car and driving, his head tried to warn him to slow down. Play it safe. It was risky to let someone else into their lives, especially for his vulnerable daughter.

In the backseat of his car, Chelsea strained against the seat belt and leaned forward. "We had so much fun today, Dad."

He looked at his daughter in the rearview mirror. "What'd you do?"

"Not much, I guess. But even helping Faith at work is so much more fun than watching Kristy with her nose in a book."

Faith angled in her seat to look at Chelsea. "I wish you were old enough for me to hire you."

"Maybe once I'm sixteen."

Gabe fisted his hands around the steering wheel. "Oh, please, don't remind me you'll be driving before I know it."

Chelsea's only answer was a delighted laugh. When they arrived at the church, they carried the food inside.

The church fellowship hall bustled with activity. Two long rectangular tables stretched end to end to hold food. Round tables filled the rest of the room. Men gathered in small groups to converse while the women darted around arranging the food and serving utensils.

It had been years since he'd attended a church dinner, but he didn't feel as fish-out-of-water as he had expected. The sounds and smells took him right back to a familiar place. And though the memories of family dinner in the fellowship hall hurt, they were comforting, as well.

As soon as they added their contribution among the platters of fried chicken and casserole dishes, Faith grabbed his arm. "Come on. Over here."

Before he could blink, she'd dragged him to a table where she proceeded to plop herself down. Across from Hannah and her four kids.

"Oh, hi, Hannah. Mind if we join you?" she asked as if she wasn't already seated.

"No, please do." Her gaze skimmed Faith, but then jumped directly to him. "Hi, Gabe. Hi, Chelsea. Have a seat."

Chelsea seemed surprised, so he knew this apparent repeat matchmaking attempt was totally Faith's doing.

But what could he do? Walk away? "Thanks."

Chelsea sat by Faith so that it left one seat open—beside Hannah. He forced a smile as he sat. He imagined he looked like someone who'd just eaten a lemon.

How could Faith do this to him? Right when he'd

thought she was interested in him, had thought he might be able to pursue some sort of…something.

But he'd misread her interest. She only wanted to fix him up with Hannah. Or someone. *Anyone.*

Faith pointed across the room. "Oh, look. There's Miss Ann, and she's sitting all alone. I think I'll move over there."

Ann didn't appear to be alone to Gabe. A man was leaning over, talking to her. But in a flash, Faith was gone—leaving Gabe to converse with a woman and her children. Albeit a beautiful woman.

But not the woman he now realized he wanted. Or at least thought he might want.

Hannah gestured to the collection of kids around the table. "Gabe and Chelsea, I'm not sure if you've ever met all my children." She introduced the four of them—six-year-old twins, seven-year-old son, and a nine-year-old daughter.

"Nice to meet all of you," Gabe said, grateful that the pastor quieted the crowd for a blessing, ending the awkward moment Faith had created.

Once they went through the food line and returned to the table, Gabe noticed the man who'd been talking to Ann now sat at the table with Faith and Ann. Seemed like he remembered seeing him before—maybe Ann's grandson.

The man sure seemed interested in Faith, who hung on his every word—except for the few times she looked over at Gabe's table and smiled.

As if satisfied with her matchmaking job.

Acid roiled in his stomach. He lost all interest in pot roast.

"So Gabe, I hear you rescued Faith from a robber the other night." Hannah gave a strained smile as she tried to break up a minor food fight between the twins. It appeared they were playing tug-of-war over a roll.

"Um, yes. Fred and I made the arrest."

Her pretty green eyes sparkled as she leaned his direction. But then one of the twins screeched at about two hundred decibels.

Mortification strained Hannah's smile into a grimace. "I'm sorry." She hopped up and hurried over to separate the twins, placing one right beside Chels—who then proceeded to roll her eyes at him.

Be nice, he mouthed to his daughter.

Chelsea had been watching Hannah and him through the whole meal, and even though he couldn't read her expression, he assumed she was pleased Faith had paired them.

He, on the other hand, was not pleased. The dinner went on interminably. The pastor spoke about the importance of youth ministry. Some high schoolers sang as they passed a basket for donations to help fund retreat scholarships and the upcoming mission trip. Then Gary and Audra told how much the kids had meant to them. Audra cried as she said they would miss everyone.

As soon as they finished speaking, Hannah touched his arm. Then she gripped her necklace as if it were a lifeline. "I wanted you to be the first to know that I'm going to be the other youth counselor. I heard about the need and felt led to volunteer."

"Cool," Chelsea said, even though he was pretty sure she wasn't supposed to hear Hannah.

Could this be another ploy of Faith's? "That's great," he felt compelled to say.

As Hannah and Chelsea chatted about the youth group, he glanced over and saw Ann's grandson laughing and leaning way too close to Faith. The man was about their age, tall, with sandy blond hair, dressed in casual—expensive—clothes.

Faith seemed to bask in his attention.

"I've agreed to help out on Sunday nights," Hannah said. "Chelsea, I look forward to getting to know you and your friends better."

Chelsea elbowed him. "Hey, Dad, I really want to go on the rafting trip that's coming up."

Focus, Gabe. He looked at his daughter. "Excuse me?"

"The retreat and rafting trip. I want to go. And I want you to go, too. You and Miss Hannah could chaperone together, and maybe we can talk Faith and Ben into going." She gave him a hundred-watt smile.

"No, Chels. You're not old enough."

"Pastor Phil said I'm old enough. And you'd be there the whole time. Miss Hannah, wouldn't you let Becca go if she were my age?"

Her pleasant expression grew strained as she

zipped the necklace pendant back and forth along the chain. “Well, I guess maybe I would. As long as I could chaperone.”

“See, Dad. You should do it.”

He shook his head and wished like crazy he could just get out of there and end this horrible scheme of Faith’s. “White-water rafting is too dangerous.”

“But Gary said it’s a beginner’s route. Only class-two rapids. And one big one at the end, maybe class three.”

They classified them? “Chels, honey, anything that needs classifying isn’t safe.” His frustration level had hit about a class nine out of ten. “Well, Hannah…kids, it’s been fun. But I need to get back to work.”

He grabbed Chelsea’s plate and piled it on top of his. Stacked their empty cups. Then he nodded his goodbye to Hannah and family.

Chelsea caught up with him at the kitchen. “You really could try harder, you know. I can tell Hannah likes you, and if you’re not interested in her, well—” she crossed her arms and looked off into the distance “—there’s always Faith.”

Uh-oh, dangerous territory. All this crazy scheming had given Chelsea false hopes. “You and Faith should leave well enough alone.”

She slung her arms out in frustration. “I’m going to the car.” She stomped away, leaving him to have to go round up Faith.

Great.

He had half a mind to just go sit and wait in the car. But he didn't have the time. So he walked over to the table where lean-in guy invaded Faith's space. Gabe's hands itched to separate the two of them.

Instead, he politely nodded to Ann and the grandson. "Evenin'. Faith, are you about ready to go?"

"Oh, Gabe, you probably remember my grandson, Daniel Foreman," Ann said. "Daniel, this is Police Chief Reynolds."

The man gave Gabe's hand a firm shake. "Nice to see you again, Gabe. I was just talking with Faith about her son, Ben. I've been reading about him and the tournament in the Atlanta paper."

He looked at the man through narrowed eyes. "Small world. Or have you two met before?"

"No, I just recognized Ben's name when she mentioned him. Pretty exciting stuff with him being listed as a hot prospect in *Sports Illustrated.* The kid has a shot at the big leagues."

"I had no idea." He looked at Faith as he said it, surprised at the disappointment eating at him. He'd thought they were friends. But Faith hadn't told him as much about her son's baseball career as she'd apparently told this stranger in one meal.

"Yes, it is time to go," Faith said. "Ann, I'll see you tomorrow. Daniel, I enjoyed having dinner with you."

"I hope we can do it again sometime."

Gabe couldn't read Faith's expression. Didn't have a clue as to whether she was interested or not.

Which burned him up all the more.

He smiled and motioned for her to go before him. He'd bite his tongue off before he'd say anything about being disappointed she hadn't talked with him more about Ben.

Yes, he was jealous. Or maybe not so much jealous as, well…jealous.

"Let's not forget the dishes," she said as she wound between the tables.

How had he possibly thought there might be some mutual attraction between them?

She hadn't told him her son was such a hot prospect.

And she'd dumped him on Hannah.

And she'd hightailed it out of there to go sit with *Daniel.*

When they reached the food tables, Faith looked up at him and jammed her hands on her hips. "What's wrong with *you?* You look like you swallowed a bullfrog and are about to croak at any moment." Then she broke the tension with a little laugh and shake of her head.

He wanted to kiss her. Right there in front of everyone.

And that was absolutely insane.

He grabbed her empty pot and bowl. "There's not a thing wrong with me." Then he stalked away from the maddening woman and headed outside to his car.

* * *

Faith took a couple of minutes to gather her dirty pie pans and cake holder—as well as gather her wits. Because surely she was hallucinating. She'd thought for one brief moment that Gabe was jealous of her talking to Daniel.

But she'd been mistaken. He was probably just irritated that she'd paired him with Hannah.

She'd seen Hannah sitting there and realized it was the perfect chance for Hannah and Gabe to get to know each other better, to see what a great match they'd be.

Faith had been getting entirely too close to Chelsea and Gabe. And this setup with Hannah had to be the answer. No more longing for something Faith couldn't have. She would force herself out of the picture by forcing Hannah into it.

Of course, Faith had spent the better part of the evening glancing over to Gabe's table, trying her best to be hopeful for the two of them hitting it off. Then hating that fact that she could hardly stand to watch them sit beside each other and talk.

And then there was Daniel. Why had Ann pushed him on her? Ann had shown excitement over Faith and Gabe making a match. And even though Faith knew it wasn't possible, she'd had a spark of hope over Ann's musings.

So why had Ann invited her grandson and then pushed him on Faith? Did she know, intuitively, that Faith wasn't right for Gabe?

"Faith?" Daniel tapped her on the shoulder.

She jumped, startled, because she'd been so caught up in her own mind she hadn't noticed his approach. "Oh, hi again."

"I'll be coming back to take care of my grandmother after her shoulder surgery. And since I'll be around for a few days, I was wondering if you'd like to go out to dinner sometime."

He smiled, and he really was handsome. And sweet to care for his granny. But he seemed to be more a fan of Ben than of her. "That's nice of you to offer. But I'm really busy at work right now, hiring and training. Plus planning for my son's visit. Maybe another time."

His frown-smile said he could tell she was giving him the brush-off. "Sure. Another time." He gave her a friendly wave, then walked back to where he proceeded to help Ann out of her seat. Such a nice man.

Not Gabe. Not Gabe, flashed in her mind like a neon sign.

And there lay the crux of the problem. She wanted Gabe. And she couldn't have him.

She squeezed her eyes closed against tears and swallowed back the wave of disappointment. She seemed to always want what she couldn't have.

Lord, am I never going to find happiness?

She was selfish and small even thinking it. But it was how she honestly felt. Like happiness was always just out of her reach.

She forced her feet to move and a smile to her lips, and she walked out the door and toward the parking lot. Gabe stood outside his squad car talking on his cell phone.

How on earth could she totally focus on Ben when Gabe was in her life just about every day now?

Lord, help me to have faith in Your plan for my life. Even when I'm falling for a man who won't ever love me back.

Chapter Ten

Later that night when Gabe got off his shift, he drove slowly home, relishing the victory. They'd been called in to help a neighboring town and had caught a prowler red-handed. Possibly the same man who'd been sniffing around the Emerson place before.

Yep. Success tasted good.

And he'd been able to forget about Faith for a few hours. A nice benefit.

But now as he wound around the curve and down their street, shadowed trees looming overhead, his thoughts zoomed in on one thing.

She was at his house. Had put his child to bed. Probably even fed her a snack and dried her hair. Filling the role of a mother for his daughter.

Even though Tina had been gone five years, guilt gnawed at him, trying to erase the thoughts of Faith. But he couldn't shake Faith from his mind.

Tina, I feel so lost without you. And Chelsea is

missing out on so much. Is it wrong to want these things for her?

Worse, what about the things he was starting to want for himself?

He climbed out of the car and walked around to the back of the house. Now he'd have to face a few minutes alone with Faith. Should he ask her about Ben? About why she hadn't told him much about her son?

He'd never been so confused, so unsure of himself, in his life. He had grown to care for this woman, yet her secrecy set off warning signals.

When he walked up on the back porch and peeked in the door and found her standing on a chair dusting the top of his refrigerator, the doubts flew right out of his head. This was Faith—his perfectionist friend. Caring. Generous. Kind. She couldn't harbor horrible secrets.

A grin spread across his face. He had to get to know this woman better.

When she heard the door open, she turned and froze. "Oh, hi, Gabe. I hope you don't mind."

"Not at all. I appreciate it. I'm sure it needed a good dusting." He reached out a hand to help her down.

She took hold, her touch sending his pulse racing, and stepped to the floor. "Did you have a good night?"

"Sure did. I'm late because we apprehended a guy who works for the newspaper and has been targeting the empty homes of subscribers who put their paper on hold."

"I'm so glad you caught him. Nice work." She lunged as if she might hug him. But at the last second, she wrapped her arms around herself instead.

He smirked. Couldn't help himself. "I wouldn't mind that congratulatory hug."

Her blush intensified, but she smiled nonetheless. "Of course." She stepped awkwardly in his direction, then tentatively wrapped her arms around his waist. "Congratulations."

She was as stiff as his nightstick. Before she could pull away from him, though, he put his arms around her and leaned down a bit so his cheek rested against the top of her head. "Thank you. And thanks for watching Chelsea for me."

He didn't let go. She felt too good in his arms. And even though he knew she wasn't truly interested in him, he still had hopes.

Letting her back away a bit, he held loosely to her waist, afraid she might bolt out the door. "Sit with me on the back porch?"

After she reached for a ponytail that wasn't there, she said, "I really should go. Maybe another time."

"I see you still haven't adjusted to your new hairstyle. But I like it. I also apologized to Chelsea and told her I like hers, as well."

She stepped out of the circle of his arms. "I know that meant a lot to her."

He wanted to get to know Faith better, maybe even ask some of the questions he had about her son. "Come on. Join me for a few minutes." He tipped his head toward the back porch.

"I guess I don't have to be in a huge hurry."

As he followed her outside, she sat on the edge of one of the wicker chairs. Between the moonlight and light from the kitchen spilling out the glass panes in the door, he could see she was perched as if ready to flee at any moment.

"You seem nervous." He sat in a chair opposite the small patio table. Far enough that he couldn't touch her, because every time he did, he let emotions take over and couldn't focus.

"I guess I am. Our friendship seems to have… changed." Her gaze shot to his.

The instant it connected with his, his insides knotted. Their relationship had changed. He just had no idea where that change was headed. "I asked you to stay because I'd like to get to know you better. That's all." No, that wasn't all. He should at least be honest. "And, well…I've wondered why you haven't told me as much about Ben as you told Daniel."

She tensed. "It wasn't intentional. I guess I don't want people to think I'm bragging about him."

"Well, his success is exciting. We—and I mean everyone in town—would like to share that with you."

Hurt tugged her features into a frown. "You know

I'm an outsider here. No one wants to hear me go on and on about Ben. They don't even know him."

"I want to hear about what's important to you," he said and then wondered if he should have been so blunt. He cleared his throat. "So what colleges are giving him a look?"

"Just about all of them. Of course, I'm pretty much left out of the loop. Every time I try to help, he tells me his dad and his coach have it under control." Pain laced through her voice.

"I'm sorry."

She stared at him. And in the moonlight, he thought he saw tears shimmer in her eyes. "Don't be so nice."

Oh, man. He couldn't take tears. So he laughed. "Okay. You want me to be mean instead?"

She smiled. "Yes. Please be a jerk so I won't be tempted to lean on you for support."

"Sorry. I don't think I could be a jerk if I tried." He winked at her. "Of course, I was a jerk earlier this evening. Thinking all kinds of uncharitable thoughts about Daniel."

The quip, meant to lighten the moment, hung between them as heavy as the humid night air, revealing his jealousy. Revealing that he had started to care.

Coiled tension sprung her from the chair. "I should go close the café."

There was nothing like revealing his true feelings to kill the moment. He walked her around the house. Moonlight streamed down, lighting the path to her car. Only the quiet night sounds joined their footfalls on the damp grass as he racked his brain, trying to figure out how to fix his blunder. Maybe if he refocused on Ben…

While she unlocked her door, he said, “So why does Ben live with his dad?”

Her hand froze midtwist. Then she continued unlocking it and slowly removed the key. “You know how I told you his grades were plummeting, and he was getting in trouble?”

“Yes.”

She stared at the door handle. “Well, I decided to let him try living at his dad’s house for a while. Ben knew some boys in the neighborhood there. Had made friends over the summer. They were good kids. A good influence.”

“So Ben did better once he moved there?”

Her hand hovered over the door handle. “Yes. A total turnaround.” She yanked open the door and was about to get in.

He stopped her, then he lifted her chin to make her look him in the eye. “You did the right thing.”

“It was really the only choice.”

But the pain in her eyes told him it was the most awful choice. He wasn’t sure he could make such a choice. And he imagined she doubted herself all the time. He ran his thumb over her cheek, wanting to offer comfort. “You’re a good mom.”

She closed her eyes and shook her head. "Please don't say that," she whispered. "You have no idea."

He waited until she opened her eyes. But the fear he saw there made his gut clench. "What happened?"

Staring toward the darkened street, she pulled away from him and seemed to weigh the decision about whether to tell him.

As he was about to repeat the question, she took a deep breath, and then she slowly let it out. "He begged for two years to go live with his dad. But I wouldn't let him. I didn't trust Walt, despite the fact he seemed to have finally settled down and was doing well for himself." With arms crossed in front of her, she glanced into his eyes. "The whole time I fought the inevitable, Ben went downhill. My anger at Walt—and my stubbornness...selfishness—nearly cost Ben his life."

He didn't dare say a word. She needed to get this all out. So he waited while she swallowed and composed herself.

"Ben was already experimenting with drugs when Walt threatened to go to court for full custody if I didn't let Ben try living there full-time." A cold, pained smile distorted her beautiful lips. "So really, there was no choice at all." She threw her purse in the car and once again tried to retreat inside. "I am not a good mom."

He pulled her hand from its tight grip on the steering wheel. He had no idea what he could say. Words couldn't help. But he had to try.

As he gently pulled her out of the car, he said, "I'm sure you did the best you could in an impossible situation."

She shook her head even as she looked into his eyes. He recognized that look. Desperation. He'd seen it often enough in the mirror.

"Listen to me, Faith. I wasn't there, but I can tell you what I see now. A woman who loves her son. Who is kind and caring to the youth at our church. And who's been a lifesaver to me as a mother figure for Chelsea." Hoping she'd believe his sincerity, he caressed her cheek. "You *are* a good mother."

She leaned into his hand and closed her eyes. Something tickled his palm and he realized it was a tear.

Oh, Lord, help me, here. She's in so much pain. Give me the words...

He caressed the other side of her face with his other palm, bracketing her face in his hands. "So you made a mistake. But Faith, honey, you ultimately did what you had to do. You were brave and unselfish. I can't imagine how hard it was to give him up."

"He was my life. And I still hurt over it every day when I can't go wake him and cook him breakfast. When I can't tuck him in bed at night or..." Her voice wavered.

"Oh, Faith," he whispered. Then he touched his lips to hers. He wanted to make it all better. To kiss away the pain. To make her forget for just a minute or two…

But the touch of their lips wasn't sweet comfort to him. It was like a torch to kindling.

He angled his head, pulled her closer, deepened the kiss. She whimpered and threw her arms around his neck, as if pouring all her pain into the kiss, into him, for him to help bear it.

Stunned, he broke away. Or had it been her pulling back first?

Too much.

Too fast.

"I'm sorry," she said as she gasped for air.

He felt the same breathlessness. His brain begged for oxygen. "No, I'm sorry." *Breathe, Gabe. Breathe.* "My fault."

Too impossible. Bad timing.

He'd just kissed the woman who was trying to fix him up with someone else. A woman in terrible emotional pain. Where was his brain in all that?

"Thank you for listening. But I have to go." Her eyes were huge, and she looked as if she was in shock.

"Okay. But it's late. Be extra cautious." Oh, man, he sounded like a robocop.

"Yes. I'll be fine. Good night. I'll see you tomorrow. For doughnuts?" She was totally serious. No teasing in her tone or expression.

"Of course. Can't go a day without my coffee and doughnuts." Again, he sounded like a recording.

Some robot talking to a near stranger. Not a man who had just kissed a woman who'd shared her deepest pain—whom he was falling hard for.

You are so lame, Gabe Reynolds. So lame.

Faith shut herself in her car and somehow managed to start the engine.

She'd just told Gabe her darkest secret. Shown him the worst of her flawed self.

How could she have done this? How had she allowed herself to say all that, and then, worse, to once again throw herself at him?

The man was simply trying to comfort her, and she'd once again thrown her arms around his neck and had practically choked him while she whimpered.

Whimpered!

Mortification scalded her face and chest.

When she stopped at the end of the street, she thumped her head into the headrest. No, no, no. She had not just done that.

Gabe kissed me.

Her stomach sprouted wings and tried to flutter away…along with her common sense.

He'd apologized. It was a mistake.

A big, fat, huge mistake.

But the worst of it was that now he knew. After a night to digest all she'd said, he would conveniently quit bringing Chelsea by. Would suddenly find the perfect babysitter for split shift nights. Might even decide he didn't need his daily coffee and doughnuts.

He *knew.* And now everyone would know her shameful past. Would know she'd failed as a mother. Would understand why her son never came around.

It wasn't that Ben was busy. It was that he didn't want to have anything to do with his mother.

When Faith arrived at the café, she squeezed her eyes shut. She refused to shed one more tear over her mess of a life. Maybe if all went well with Ben, and Gabe and the other townsfolk could see them together, she'd have a chance to show she *could* be a good mother.

She tried dialing Ben one more time. It went straight to voice mail, and she had the sick feeling that her hopes for healing their broken relationship were ridiculously naive.

Gabe had to fix it. Had to fix the situation with Faith. He'd hardly slept a wink last night, but at least he had a plan to show for it. A constructive plan to help Faith. Not something as stupid as his idiotic move last night.

He stood at the stove, rinsing the coffeepot, when Chelsea came dragging in wearing her pajamas and poured herself some cereal and milk.

"Chels, I've decided to take the morning off."

"Really?" She didn't look convinced he'd do it.

But she still waited with her spoon hovering over the bowl of Cheerios as if hopeful.

"Yep. Fred offered to cover for me today, and I'm taking him up on it."

"Awesome. What are we going to do?" She scooped a spoonful of cereal and began to munch.

"Just hang out. Although I'd like to run by to talk to Faith."

"Cool," she said, then slurped up milk that dribbled out while talking with her mouth full.

"Watch your manners." His lips tilted upward since it was tough to be stern when she looked so cute in her pink pajamas with bed-head.

She smiled and chewed as he joined her at the table.

"Chels, you know Faith's son, Ben, is coming for a visit, right?"

She nodded. "But it's kind of weird that he doesn't come more often. It seems like all he does is play baseball. Poor Faith must feel left out."

"Yes. So this visit is very important to her. I'd like for us to do all we can to help welcome Ben. So he'll like it here."

Her brown eyes nearly glowed with excitement as she hurriedly chewed and swallowed. "Maybe we can invite them over or something."

Pleased to see she had a sense of the situation as well as compassion for Faith, he patted his daughter's hand. "Good idea. As soon as you're finished, let's head over to the café."

She ate and dressed in record time, and before the hour was up, they strolled into the Coffee Time Café. Even though he'd already eaten, the aroma of freshly baked cinnamon rolls made his mouth water.

"Can I help you?" Faith said from somewhere behind the counter.

"The question is, can we help you?" he replied.

Faith popped around from behind the coffee machine as if surprised. Her face drained of color, then a flood of pink followed.

The kiss. He'd embarrassed her last night. Maybe if he acted as if nothing happened, it would ease the tension. "Hi."

"Hi, you two. What brings you by?"

"Dad's off today. And we've got a plan," Chelsea said in a singsong voice. "Oh, there's Miss Ann!" She headed toward the table. "You two talk. I need to check in with my prayer partner."

Once Chelsea settled across the room, Faith and he were forced to look at each other once again.

She smiled.

He smiled back.

Awkward.

"So what's this plan Chelsea mentioned?"

He nodded toward a table. "Can we talk?"

Dread. It was the only way to describe the expression on her face. She nodded and joined him as if expecting bad news.

As he sat across from her and looked into her

aqua-colored eyes, flashes of the previous night darted through his mind. Sharing her pain. Kissing her soft lips. "It's not a big deal," he said, talking about his plan as well as trying to convince himself the same about that amazing kiss. "Chelsea and I would like to have you and Ben over while he's in town."

She gripped her hands together on the table—the knuckles turning white. "That's nice of you to offer."

Trying to ease her tension, he rested his hand over hers. "I want to do anything I can to help…well, you know. To make the visit easier. So if you're having a hard time talking, or he's shutting down…just call. And you know Chelsea. She's never met a stranger." Suddenly feeling silly, he looked away, hoping he hadn't offended her with the offer. "We just want to help. Any way you need."

"Well…" She swallowed hard, then blinked several times.

Oh, great. He'd blown it. "Faith, I'm sorry if—"

"No." She shook her head. "It's the nicest thing anyone's done for me in a long time." She glanced away, then her gaze once again settled on him. "Thank you. I'd like that. And I promise to let you know if we get in a tough spot."

"Good." He relaxed back in his chair, relieved to have the conversation out of the way. And wondering when he'd started caring so much about his neighbor's happiness.

She seemed to relax as well and returned an easy smile. "You know, I'll owe you big-time if you can help me keep him here for two weeks. His visit last summer got preempted by a school trip to Europe."

Her pronouncement slammed into him like a sucker punch, but he didn't let the pain—or anger—show. "That was a big opportunity. Couldn't the visit have been rescheduled?"

"They tried. We ended up arranging that I would take him to an out-of-state tournament later in the summer. But, as you can imagine, we didn't spend nearly enough time together.

"It's not my place to say anything, but Walt should make the visits happen."

Pain etched itself in her face—brows drawn together, a worry wrinkle between her eyes that he wished he could banish. She sighed. "I wish I could say Walt is the trouble. But he's been as baffled as I've been about Ben's resistance to visiting. The older Ben gets, the more he pulls away."

Gabe wasn't willing to let Walt off the hook so easily, but what could he do? "Let's just assume all will turn out well this year." Time to change the subject to one he could control. "Hey, would you be willing to help me with Chelsea's big birthday coming up?"

Her smile said she was grateful for the new discussion. "The thirteenth should be a big one."

The thought of his baby becoming a teenager…

well, he didn't want to go there yet. He still had a couple of weeks to deal with it. "I need gift suggestions."

"Jewelry. Or perfume," she said without hesitation. "Something feminine would mean a lot." She glanced out the shop window and stared at something in the distance. "I could help you shop for her if you'd like."

Whoa. He'd come to offer help. Not to solicit her help on a shopping trip. "Thanks. I may take you up on that."

There, that was noncommittal. He would have some time to figure out exactly what he wanted where Faith was concerned.

Take it slow. Test the waters. Be smart.

She fiddled with the flowers. Arranging them, turning the vase, then starting over again. "I guess I should check on Juanita."

"Okay, I won't keep you."

"Thanks, Gabe. For everything." Her smile didn't have its usual sparkle. Had his noncommittal reply hurt her feelings?

Oh, man. He was such a heel. She'd offered to help with a motherly-type thing and he'd rejected it. He'd hit her where she was most sensitive. Most vulnerable.

"You know, Faith, I *could* use a friend to help me shop for Chel's birthday gift. I've not done well with the party thing. I really want to do it right this year."

Her fists clenched, then released. "Of course. We'll trade services and help each other with our children." Her smile still didn't make it all the way to shine mode. But it was an improvement.

Faith was touched by Gabe's offer but hurt that his first reaction to her attempt to help him had been to brush it off. Maybe now that he knew the truth about her, he was doing exactly what she'd feared and was pulling away.

But surely he wouldn't have offered to help with Ben if he were truly pulling away. Of course helping with Ben was one thing. Allowing Faith access to Chelsea was something else entirely.

He scooted his chair back and waved at his daughter across the café. "Chels, I'm going to run to the hardware store. You wanna go?"

"No, thanks. I'll wait here."

Faith watched him head out the door, his broad shoulders pretty much filling the entire doorway. Broad, strong shoulders she'd wrapped around last night. She sucked in air once again as if he'd just kissed her senseless.

"Hey, Faith, come here a second," Chelsea called. "Miss Ann and I need you."

Oh, boy. More matchmaking. She was sure of it. And she wasn't up for it.

As soon as she sat, Chelsea leaned close. "It didn't go well last night."

Last night? Panic squeezed her chest. Had Chelsea

seen them outside? "What?" she squeaked through spasmodic airways like an asthmatic having an attack.

"Dad hardly gave Hannah the time of day at the dinner."

Last night. The dinner. Hannah.

Air rushed back into her lungs. "Oh, the dinner. Yes. I wondered about that."

"So, what did you think of my grandson?" Ann asked. "He sure seemed taken with you."

It sounded like some kind of test, which still baffled her. "Oh, he's really nice. I'm glad he'll be here to help after your shoulder surgery."

"I see. So no dates lined up with Daniel?"

"Um…no. Not a moment of free time." But would it be such a bad idea? Maybe it would help take her mind off Gabe.

Chelsea waved her hand in front of their faces. "Come on, people. Back to the topic at hand. My dad." She rested her chin on her fists and frowned. "I think maybe we pushed too hard last night."

Relieved that maybe Chelsea would relent and forget this whole stupid plan, she said, "Then let's just stay out of it and see what happens."

"No way." Chelsea crossed her arms and pasted a stubborn look on her face. "I'm not giving up so easily."

Ann squinted at Faith through suspicious eyes—eyes that also held a gleam of excitement. "Yes, we could let God work and watch what happens. That sounds like a good plan to me."

There was the God-working thing again. *Lord, please take away this false hope I have. Please take away any feelings I have for Gabe. Bring him the woman You have planned for him.*

And help me mean every word of this.

Chelsea sighed. "I say forget Hannah. Let's work on someone new."

Ann's attention finally moved to Chelsea. "Someone who has some chemistry with your dad?"

"Yeah. I can tell he doesn't feel much for Hannah."

A little thrill flitted through Faith. No chemistry between him and Hannah, huh? "Any ideas who might be a fit?" she asked just to add to the conversation.

Chelsea picked at a hangnail. "You know what I really want." Her eyes darted to Faith's. "But you're just friends," she said with a whine as if mimicking Faith's earlier statement.

"Yes, friends." And maybe if she said it enough, she would convince herself.

Ann struggled out of her chair. "Oh, I think I know someone who would be a good fit."

Chelsea looked from Ann to Faith, then back to Ann. She clapped her hands while doing a wiggly dance in her chair. "Is it Faith? Come on, tell me!"

"I think I'll just keep that to myself and watch what happens." Ann winked at Faith. "I'll see you two tomorrow." She hobbled out of the café with a slow *thump, thump* of her cane.

Launching herself halfway across the table, Chelsea grabbed Faith's hands. "Is it you? Do you like my dad—you know, as a boyfriend?"

Faith could barely breathe. She couldn't let Chelsea get her heart set on the idea. She gave Chelsea's hands a quick squeeze, then let go. "I think she's teasing. Let's just keep praying and wait."

Hurt flashed in Chelsea's eyes. But then she seemed to throw up a barrier, and all the fire fled from her pretty brown eyes. Chelsea acted as if Faith had rejected her as well as Gabe. "Well, if you don't want to date my dad, I'm going to be looking for someone else. I won't give up."

What would Chelsea think if she knew her dad had kissed Faith?

Another reason to keep her distance from the Reynoldses. And maybe another reason to take Daniel up on his dinner invitation.

Chapter Eleven

As Gabe relaxed on the back porch after dinner that evening, he realized he was doubly blessed. Not only was his daughter smart and mostly well behaved, but she was also just plain fun to be around.

He'd failed to enjoy her company often enough and planned to rectify the situation.

He stood, stretched and admired the orange-pink rays of the sun as it headed westward. Then he went inside to check on Chelsea. He found her hovered over her desk, writing.

She paused and tapped the pen on the desktop. "I decided to send Ben a note to welcome him to Corinthia."

The sight of her working so hard to be thoughtful tightened his chest. "I'm proud of you for jumping in to help Faith."

"Hey, Dad, I need you to get Ben's address."

He ruffled her short hair—a style that now seemed to fit her perfectly. A pretty good sign that he was moving forward. "I'll run next door and get it for you." He grabbed the envelope.

"Can't you just call?" She grinned at him, and he imagined her matchmaking wheels turning.

"I needed to talk to Faith anyway." He tried to look all business as he left the house when he had no excuse other than the fact he wanted to see her.

She didn't answer on the first knock, so he went to the back door. When she answered, she wore rubber gloves and held a toothbrush. "Come in."

"Doing some heavy dental cleaning?"

She smiled. "Just cleaning the grout."

"That's a relief." He laughed as she peeled off the gloves. "So, I've noticed you're a perfectionist."

"I suppose I am where housework is concerned."

"I'd say you're just as hard on yourself."

She pointed at the envelope, skirting the issue. "What's that for?"

He handed it to her. "Chels wanted to send Ben a note to welcome him, and we need his address."

She hesitated and he thought she would refuse. "That's sweet of her. But..."

"Only if it's okay with you, though."

She had a desk in the corner of the kitchen. There was a blue wire bill sorter with a matching file holder. An address book lay off to the side, although she didn't open it.

She took a pen out of a blue wire cup and wrote Ben's name and the Atlanta address. "Of course it's okay. I guess I'm just anxious about him coming. I still haven't reached him since the tournament final. If they won, it could throw a wrench in our plans."

"We'll hope for the best." He took the envelope and slipped it in his back pocket but didn't really want to leave yet. He moved toward the back door anyway. "See you Sunday, I guess."

She shoved her hands into the back pockets of old, tattered jeans that had several bleached-out spots—her cleaning jeans, apparently. "Oh, before you go. I wanted to let you know I loved my afternoon interviewee. I offered him the part-time position."

"Great news."

"Yes, everything is working out after all." She followed him out to the porch.

He wasn't sure what else to say. Or to do. So he started down the steps.

"You know, things seem to be looking up. And while I was scrubbing the floor tonight, I had this sense that God has everything under control. That good things are coming."

He stopped a couple of steps below her and turned. They were nearly eye to eye. Just a little space between them. "I'm glad. You deserve it."

"I've been praying for Ben's visit for a long time—ever since he missed his summer visit last year."

The Europe trip. Made him angry just thinking about it. "Well, I'll pray, too, if you'd like."

She tilted her head. "Would you?"

He'd been praying more since he'd been around Faith. And since attending church. "Sure."

"Are you still mad at God?"

The question jolted him. "Why would you think I'm mad at God?"

"With Tina's death and all. And since I got angry with God over my husband leaving me with a new baby, I just assumed…."

"So that's how it happened? Walt walked out on you and Ben?"

She nodded, matter-of-factly, as if she'd dealt with the pain long ago. "He was a freshman in college and felt tied down. Went to parties to escape the pressure. Etcetera, etcetera…and to be fair, I probably screeched at him about one thing or another every time he walked in the door."

"You were both so young."

She shrugged. "Young. And angry. At him and at God."

It was difficult to think back to when Tina died, to right after the accident. A dark time. "I'm not really sure if I was mad at God. I just checked out. Stayed at Chelsea's hospital bedside until I knew she would make it, but that time is a blur."

"I'm glad you're praying now, Gabe. It'll help you through the teenage years with Chelsea—"

"Which is already a lot easier thanks to you." He had to touch her. To somehow show her how he felt. Even though he didn't really know yet how he felt.

She seemed frozen in place, hands still tucked safely in her back pockets, so he ran his hand along the length of her upper arm, up and down. As if he were trying to warm her. "I appreciate all the help you've given me with my daughter. We may just make it through this burst of independence."

She smiled. But she didn't move. Didn't touch him back. "So have you thought any more about buying that new couch?"

"No." *But I've thought of you every single day while you seem more interested in my furniture than in me.* "Chelsea turning thirteen is all the change I need right now."

How could he want to kiss her when she radiated *keep away* vibes?

She moistened her lips, then took a step back. "You'll both survive thirteen. I'm sure of it. Now—" she gestured toward the back door "—I have a pile of dirty laundry calling my name."

Her hands were finally out of the pockets. But he could take a hint. He moved on down the steps, away from her warmth. From the comfort of her sweet perfume mixed with a hint of fresh, clean Pine-Sol. "Thanks for the address."

Nope. There was no way her arms were going around him tonight. Apparently, she'd come to the conclusion last night was a mistake.

And hadn't it been?

If she had no interest in him, then surely it was a mistake. Better to know now than to make another dumb move and force her to have to politely reject him.

But he cared about her already. And he had no idea how to handle it.

When he arrived home, all was quiet except for the sound of the shower down the hall. He found Ben's welcome note waiting for its envelope beside the pile of outgoing mail.

On it, Chelsea had handwritten a note.

Your mom talks about you all the time! She sure misses you and is so happy you're coming. We can't wait to finally meet you!! You'll have to come hang out one day to rescue me from my boring summer.

See ya soon,

Chelsea Reynolds (the kid next door).

A nice note. Maybe it would help make sure Ben didn't disappoint his mom again this summer. Because no matter how Faith felt about Gabe, she deserved a chance to reconcile with her son.

And Gabe was going to make sure she got it.

On Sunday morning, Faith woke with a new sense of purpose. She found strength in the fact she had remained strong during the last encounter with Gabe. She hadn't thrown her arms around him the other night on the back porch. And each time she ran into him over the weekend, she'd managed to maintain her distance.

Yes, her world felt more stable when she focused on her son and kept Chelsea and Gabe neatly slotted in the friend-and-neighbor category.

Faith arrived at the church early, so she stopped out front to call Ben. It rang several times, and as she was about to give up hope, he answered. Static rattled the line.

"Ben, can you hear me?"

"Barely…no signal…driving…"

"Did you win the tournament?" she yelled.

Dead space filled the silence. The kind that usually indicated a dropped call. But the display showed they were still connected. "Are you still there?"

The connection hissed and popped. "…call later." Then the call ended.

At least she had encouragement. He'd answered his phone. With a smile on her face, she slipped into the sanctuary and took her regular seat. No way was she going to wait for an invitation from Chelsea and Gabe. Plus, she didn't need Miss Ann fanning the flames of hope any more than she already had.

As the pastor walked up the aisle toward the back of the church to turn on the sound system, he stopped beside her row. "I hope you'll bring Ben next Sunday. I'd love to meet him."

"Thanks, Phil. I will."

As more folks filed into the sanctuary, she opened her bulletin to read the announcements. But all she could think about was Ben.

She hoped she'd hear back from him this time.

Sometime today would be nice. But she'd learned not to count on it. He was a busy kid. Plus, Walt had remarried and had two more children. Another reason it was difficult to spend time with

Ben. He loved his half siblings, loved his stepmom and preferred to spend time with his new family.

She thought about her life as a business owner—all the hours she was required to put in. Could she blame Ben?

And he was a tough kid to love. She would tell him she loved him, and all he ever said back was, *"You, too."*

Ben had never responded well to her telling him she loved him. He always seemed to doubt it, even when he was very young. Maybe because actions always spoke louder than words to him—just like they did for Faith.

I'll show him while he's here. I'll give him my undivided attention. I'll treat him like the special young man he is. I'll spoil him.

She couldn't wait till he arrived.

Lord, help me show him. And thank You for—

Gabe and Chelsea passed by, heading toward their seats at the front. She clutched a hand to her chest because her heart stuttered at seeing Gabe in a suit, his strong shoulders and confident gait reminding her he was sturdy and dependable.

Thank You for my new friendships here at church.

Right before they sat, he turned and scanned the crowd. He zoomed in on her immediately. Their eyes met.

She wiggled her fingers in a tentative wave. Not too exuberant. Not the giant, arm-crossing wave she wanted to do to let him know how happy she was to see him.

He tugged Chelsea's hand, and they both started back up the aisle.

Toward her.

Oh, my.

He gave her a half grin as they approached and he didn't let his gaze stray to anyone else they passed. It was as if the two of them were tethered.

And she was reeling him in.

Breathless, she froze.

"Hey," he said simply, once they reached her.

"Hey."

"Our pew or yours?" No other options. No room for declining.

"Mine," she said just as simply, in wonder at her audacity as she slid over to make room.

"Cool." Chelsea plopped down right beside Faith, leaving Gabe to sit on the end.

Once he was settled, he smiled over Chelsea's head. All that gorgeousness focused on her. With his full lips, angled smile, white teeth and shining black eyes, he pretty much stunned her senseless.

She couldn't even smile back. But luckily the pastor started speaking. *Breathe, Faith.* She dragged in a nice, deep breath so she wouldn't keel over.

Gabe had chosen to come sit with her. *Her.* Right in front of everyone.

Yes, definitely very cool. But in that one gesture,

all the walls of defense she'd carefully built over the weekend had crumbled.

Monday dawned clear and perfectly beautiful with rare low humidity. It was as if God made the day especially for Faith, just to welcome her to the new morning. To give her hope.

Three more days till Ben came. Since she hadn't heard back from him, she had to assume he was traveling home from the tournament and that all was on schedule. She couldn't believe the time had nearly arrived. She had so much to do. Grocery shopping. More cleaning. And today was Natalie's last day. She'd planned a small farewell party and needed to arrive early to decorate the cookie cake she'd made last night.

She hurried to get ready for work, then drove to the café. Everything seemed easier this morning. It had been easier to get up and going. Easier to head to work. And now it would be easier to wish Natalie well in her new venture because she knew Juanita and her new employee, Randy, would work out just fine.

Though Faith had had a couple of scares, it was as if God had orchestrated everything lately so that she'd have the perfect vacation with Ben.

For the first time in her adult life, she had confidence that all would work out well.

And maybe, just maybe, she'd be totally happy.

After the surprise party to wish her well, Natalie

sniffed and blinked away tears. "I'm going to miss you so much."

Faith fought her own tears. "I'll miss you. But I want you to be happy and enjoy your new life."

They hugged and then jumped right in to work when they saw a line of customers waiting for them to open. Their busiest morning yet.

Ann showed up at her regular time. "I see you're too busy to chat today." She patted Faith's hand. "We'll catch up later."

Relief made her grin and nod. "Sounds good."

Ann winked at her.

Yep. Without Chelsea around, Ann would definitely badger her about her feelings for Gabe.

Which brought the smile down a notch.

Gabe. Strong. True.

She sensed there was something between them. But she didn't see how it could work. The man wouldn't even get rid of Tina's couch. How could he possibly love her and make a total commitment—something she would desperately need?

Her cell phone vibrated, but she had to ignore it. Two more customers in line.

She wiped her forehead with her sleeve. A great morning, businesswise, but she was tired.

The café phone rang.

It could be Ben. Faith hurried to her office and grabbed the phone receiver with a smile on her face. "Coffee Time Café. This is Faith."

"It's Walt. We need to talk."

Her stomach dropped to her toes. "Is Ben okay?"

He huffed. "He's fine. Why do you always assume the worst?"

"Why do you always start off a conversation sounding like you have terrible news to bear?" She wanted to screech at him to have a brain cell and not do that to her when he knew how she worried.

Instead, she took a calming breath—often required in conversations with her ex-husband—and said, "What's up?"

"Look, Ben's team pulled it out last Monday and won in extra innings. He feels awful..."

A buzzing started in her ears.

"...was supposed to call you but..."

She dropped into her chair. Closed her eyes. *No.*

"...will be in Florida for a week for a championship tournament. We're staying a few days to take the kids to Disney World..."

They were doing it again. Baseball and the new family came first.

"...college and pro scouts. There's no way he can miss this opportunity..."

"Of course." But maybe she'd missed something. Maybe there was still a chance. "I guess we'll have to change the date of his visit. When *can* he come?"

Silence.

"Faith, I'm sorry. I don't see how Ben can make it up there this summer. It's just been so crazy with all this interest in him. Interviews and meetings and awards and—"

"Stop it." Fury that had simmered suddenly spewed. "Just stop it. I don't want excuses. I want my rights as a mother to see my son."

"We're not keeping you from seeing him. He's just too busy with his budding career to put everything on hold to come up there for two weeks."

The eruption left her drained. Her spine turned to jelly. She wanted to just lay her head on her desk and wail. "When does he leave?"

"On Wednesday."

The day he was supposed to arrive here. *Just get through this phone call.* "Will he be at your house tomorrow?"

"As far as I know. He'll have to pack."

"I'll be there to see him before dinner. Can you make sure he's home?"

"I will." He sighed. She could imagine him raking his hand through his hair. "I'm really sorry about this, Faith. I know how much—"

"Goodbye, Walt." She couldn't bear his pity. She hung up.

Rather than fall into a heap in the floor like her very bones wanted to do, she forced herself to leave the office and find Natalie.

"Nat, I need to go home. I'm not feeling well."

"Everything okay on the phone call?"

No. "Yes. Could you possibly stay and help Juanita

close?" At the moment, she didn't care what happened to the café.

"Sure. Anything to help. Call me if you're still sick tomorrow."

She had the hysterical urge to laugh. She could promise she would still feel sick tomorrow.

She'd failed as a mom. Both when Ben was a middle schooler and needed her most and again now, when she'd needed to reach out to him.

She would never have the chance to spend the time she needed to show him how much she loved him, how important he was to her. They would never recover that mother-child bond and would probably remain in this tense, superficial relationship.

She couldn't bear the thought.

Somehow, she made the drive home. She walked into the house, shut all the blinds and then curled up under a plush throw blanket on the couch.

Now, when he didn't show for the much-anticipated visit, her failures would become public. Everyone would find out the situation—that Faith was a woman whose son had chosen to live with his dad, and that, for some reason Faith couldn't figure out, he had no interest in spending time with her.

Thinking of the potential rejection from her new friends sent her back inside her cocoon. Eventually, she slept, going in and out of nightmares. She ignored the phone anytime it rang. Gabe's voice called out to her from the answering machine. At one point, someone knocked at the door. She tried to tell them to go away, but she didn't have the energy.

How could she be chilled to the bone in the dead of summer?

Chapter Twelve

Gabe couldn't stand it any longer. Why wouldn't Faith answer the door? Was she seriously ill?

Fear drove him to return to her house and try the doors. Thankfully, the front door wasn't locked. He knocked lightly as he opened it.

No sound. No lights.

But a heap lay on the couch.

"Faith?" He nearly strangled on her name as he ate up the room in three strides, then braked to a halt at her side.

She turned to look up at him. "Gabe?"

His eyes fell shut. Knees went limp. Some cop he was.

"Thank God you're okay." He flipped on a lamp. "Oh, man, you look horrible."

Instead of the laugh and *"Gee, thanks"* he expected, she stared at him, forlorn.

"Rough time, huh?" He held up a bag from the pharmacy. "Natalie called me. I brought sinus medicine, flu medicine, pain relief, saltines and ginger ale. Choose your treatment."

"Ben's not coming."

The jolt of three simple words knocked him back a step.

She huddled up once again. "Thanks for worrying about me. I'll be fine."

The sight of her tucked under that blanket, back curved so pitifully, made him ache for her.

He tossed the bag onto a chair, and then he lifted her so he could scoot in under her. He rubbed his cheek against the top of her head. "I'm so sorry."

She didn't cry. Just sat there weak as a kitten. A kitten who'd taken a beating. His own chest ached as if someone had wrenched his heart. *Why, Lord? Why, when this was the one thing she needed?*

He didn't know how long they sat like that. But after a bit, she snuggled against him as if letting go of some of the tension. But still no tears.

He brushed her hair away from her face. "How'd you find out?"

"Walt called. Ben's team won the tournament. They're going to another in Florida. With college and pro scouts."

"That's good for Ben, I guess."

She shrugged. "Yeah. I'm probably being selfish."

"No, you're not. You're just disappointed." What could he say? Nothing would make it better. Not when the one thing she'd looked so forward to had been pulled out from under her. "I'm sorry."

He shook his head at how useless platitudes were.

"Can you let people know he's not coming? I just can't face the questions."

"Sure. Don't worry about it."

She worked her hand out of the blanket and took hold of his hand. She gave it a squeeze. "Thank you. You're a good friend."

He wanted more than that, though. It went against all logic, and he had no idea what, if anything, he could do about it. But a quiet hum sang through his body and to the tips of his fingers as he knew, without a doubt, that he wanted more than friendship with Faith Hagin.

He brushed the hair behind her ear. Lifted her chin.

She looked into his eyes, and the bleakness there stopped him in his tracks.

Wrong time. She was too hurt. Too vulnerable.

So he pulled her to him once again, cradling her face to his chest. "We'll figure this out. Surely you can spend some time with your son somehow."

Her bone-weary sigh tickled his chest. "I'm driving down to see him briefly tomorrow before he leaves for Florida."

Anger at the bad timing of the tournament made him grit his teeth, even though he knew this was ultimately a positive thing for Ben. "I'm glad you're going. That's a start. Is there anything I can do?"

"No. But thanks for your support." She untangled from her blanket and stood. "I think I overindulged in a pity party today. I should go back to the café." She folded the blanket and tossed it over the back of the couch. Then she tried to straighten her hair.

"I was just there. Your employees have everything under control."

She wrapped her arms around her waist as if trying to keep warm. "Okay."

"You want me to call Chelsea to come over with Monopoly? She'd love to keep you company."

"Thanks, but I need some time to myself. To prepare for tomorrow. I'm going to offer to go to Florida with him. Although, his dad's making a family vacation out of the trip—Disney World and all. How can I compete against that?"

He got up off the couch and hugged her. "It's not a competition. Just be yourself. Remind Ben how great you are. I think he'll figure out a way to spend time with his mom."

A whisper of a smile lifted her lips. "Thanks." She looked up at him like she might be interested in that kiss, after all.

But it was just gratitude. And timing. So he released her and forced himself to put one foot in front of the other, moving toward the door. "Sorry about barging in uninvited. But Natalie told me you were sick. I was worried."

Wrapping her arms around herself once again, she said, "You were just doing your officerly duty. No harm done."

Officerly duty? If only it were as simple as that.

* * *

It wasn't merely a shower but buckets of hard, driving rain that hammered Faith's car the next evening on the way to see Ben. The nightmarish Atlanta traffic delayed her an hour.

And nearly frayed her last nerve.

When she pulled up at Walt's house, she was pleased to see Ben's truck. Walt had kept his word.

And if she were honest, she had to admit that he'd grown into a dependable man. And had a really sweet wife and cute kids. But sometimes, when he did little things like frighten her with phone calls, she couldn't help but dredge up the worst memories.

She ran, splashing water over her sandals, to the front door of their huge home that sat in a prime location of a swanky Atlanta neighborhood. Walt's success was still one thing that grated against her. Then again, she was thankful for all the advantages it offered Ben. Like his trip to Europe last summer. This trip to Disney World. And all the baseball travel that had helped him get to where he was today.

Walt's wife, Susie, answered the door. She was cute, sweet, confident. Everything Faith was not. Only Faith never had been able to dislike the woman. She was very good to Ben.

"Hi, Faith. Come on in."

"I'm sorry I'm late. Traffic."

She waved away the fact Faith was probably

delaying dinner. "No problem. Ben's up in his room packing. Top of the stairs, first door on the right."

Faith didn't really need the reminder. She'd visited with him here several times when he hadn't been able to come to her house.

Her climb up the hardwood floor staircase was muffled by an elegant runner. She found her son tucking clothes into a suitcase that was open on his bed. No more little boy bedroom. This was an adult's room with the exception of trophies lining shelves they'd built on one whole wall.

Ben startled when she tapped on his door. "Mom! I didn't hear you."

"Sorry I'm late. I hit traffic." To hug or not to hug? He usually avoided it. But she couldn't. It had been a while since she'd seen him, so she crossed the room and embraced him.

He actually hugged her back. "I'm packing."

"I see. Can you use some help?"

"I'm good, I guess."

They stood staring at each other, but he glanced away. He didn't want to look her in the eye.

He suddenly turned away and grabbed a pile of T-shirts. He stuffed it in the suitcase. "Look, I'm really sorry. I know you've been buying tickets to Braves games and stuff. I had Dad call because I didn't want to upset you."

"I know this win is a huge opportunity. But I admit I'm really disappointed we can't spend time together."

"Yeah, well…" The shirts didn't want to fit in the

space he'd allotted. He shoved at them and grunted in frustration. "I'm tired of feeling like I let you down."

His sudden anger made her jerk back as if slapped in the face. But she forced a calm she didn't feel. Ben was obviously hurting, too. "What do you mean?"

He rolled a pair of jeans. Slapped them into the bag. "It's all you could talk about—my visit. Even though you know how crazy my summer is with baseball. I *love* playing ball." His cheeks reddened as he gave her a desperate look. "I'll probably get a full ride to college. But are you excited for me? No, all you can think about is having me there. Just so you'll be happy."

"Oh, Ben. I'm excited for you. But, I love you and miss you so much."

Pain ripped through her chest. She had no words. Had no idea where this anger was coming from.

He stopped fighting with the clothes and hung his head. "I'm sorry. I just…"

She pulled him to sit beside her on the bed. "Talk to me, sweetie. Don't hold anything back. I need to understand."

He took some shallow breaths as if trying to hold back his emotion. "I know you don't mean to, but you always pressure me. To…I don't know. To be everything for you." He clenched his hands. "I feel like I can't have my own life when you're around or when I talk to you. You make me feel guilty. Because you need me so much."

"Oh, Ben."

He looked at her with troubled eyes. "Why didn't you ever date anyone when I was younger?"

Memories of all the times she'd declined second or third dates rattled around in her head. "I did, but I never brought them home. I didn't trust anyone not to hurt us."

His head fell back and he stared at the ceiling. "I never knew. All I knew was that I had to be the *man of the house*. And you depended—" His voice cracked. "You depended on me to make you happy."

She couldn't make her voice work. A fist of regret clutched her by the throat.

He looked at her then. Big tears welled up in his eyes. He shrugged, and it seemed as if he were thirteen again. "That was just too much pressure for a kid."

She hugged him, and this time, he clung to her, as well. Silent sobs racked his body. As if he didn't remember quite how to cry now that he was a man.

Could there be anything more painful than a grown son crying on her shoulder, so big he could hardly fit? She swallowed her own tears as she rubbed a hand over his soft hair. She needed to be strong for him. "Ben, I'm so sorry. I never meant to do that to you. I just wanted to protect you. And I've always been happy as long as you're happy."

"How ironic is that?" He scooted away from her,

wiped his eyes on his sleeve, then pulled his emotions together—trying once again to look cool and collected. "Don't you see? That's wrong. I know I'm your kid and all, but you need to take care of *you* now. And I'll take care of me."

She'd made her poor son miserable through his teen years, expecting him to fill a void he couldn't fill. And she hadn't even realized it.

Fingers of anguish clenched at her stomach. "Honey, I'm so sorry. I had no idea..." A sob tried to escape, but she locked it in. She had to focus on him right now. "You're still my son, the most important person in my life. But I hope you'll forgive me for pressuring you—even unintentionally."

He struggled some more to check the emotion and continued packing. No forgiveness offered. "We're going to the championship. It's huge," he said, dropping the subject.

"Your dad told me. I'd love to come to Florida to see you play." Maybe they could find some common ground. "I've got the vacation time lined up already."

His expression tensed. "I don't think I'm ready to have you and Dad together for that long in close quarters. I'll be nervous enough with the scouts there."

"Sure thing, honey. I'll come another time." She stood and began rearranging his suitcase. "Why don't you let a pro help?"

"Thanks. I hate packing." He handed her a pile of uniforms.

"You know, I'm really proud of you and all you've accomplished. I met a man at a church dinner this past week who's been following your career. He treated me like a celebrity or something."

He shook his head, embarrassed. He'd always been awkward with the attention and seemed to have stayed humble—and grateful for any success.

She opened one of the jerseys to refold it. It was huge. "When did you get so grown-up?"

He shrugged. "Little by little."

Yeah, gradual changes could sneak up on a person. Like her relationship with Gabe.

Should she tell Ben about him? She folded two pairs of pants before she got her nerve. But somehow she knew it was the right thing to do.

"You know, Ben, there's a man I've started to care for."

He seemed only the slightest bit interested as he handed her another jersey. "What's his name?"

She took a deep three-second breath—in through the nose, out through the mouth. Saying it out loud would make it pretty real. But Ben had just shared his heart with her. She could share with him. "His name is Gabe. And he's my next-door neighbor…"

Chapter Thirteen

Faith parked in her driveway, but when she saw Gabe's car in his driveway, she was drawn next door. All the way home, she'd wanted to talk to him. To share the pain of the conversation with Ben. To lean on Gabe even though she knew she shouldn't.

When he opened his front door and took one look at her, he held his arms open.

She couldn't have resisted his offer any more than she could have resisted breathing. Without a thought to how it might look to anyone on the street or to Chelsea, she stepped into his embrace.

"Tell me all about it."

"Whoa," Chelsea said from behind her dad. The lilt in her voice said it was a *good* whoa, not a *stop* whoa.

Faith forced herself to pull away from Gabe.

"How about you go to your room and let us talk," Gabe said. And Faith was pretty sure his face had reddened.

Chelsea didn't make a move. She looked at Gabe.

Then at Faith. Then at Gabe again. "It's about time." A huge grin nearly split her face. She whooped and did some sort of dance down the hallway toward her room. "God is so good," she sang. As she closed her door, she continued to belt out the song from the top of her lungs.

"Sorry about that," Gabe said.

"Not your fault. I shouldn't have come." Her face burned and it probably matched his.

He gestured outside. "Let's sit on the porch."

They sat in wicker chairs on either side of a small round table—a matching set with the furniture in back. She could imagine Tina and Gabe having a glass of sweet iced tea on the porch in evenings past.

The next thing she knew, he scooted his chair closer so they were knee to knee. It was dark and he hadn't bothered with a porch light. They were lost in their own secluded world.

He took her hand. "Tell me what happened."

His closeness made her dizzy at the same time it brought comfort. He smelled strong and dependable, if that were possible—masculine and clean with a bit of spicy added in…familiar. She grasped his hand tighter. "Ben was angry, as usual. But he finally talked to me."

"I take it that didn't go well."

Now the hard part. How could she explain the mistakes she'd made without sounding like a nutcase? "He was angry because, well, I've put too much pressure on him."

"Pressured how?"

"Basically, to make me happy." She shrugged. "And all along, I've felt horrible because I couldn't make *him* happy." Or anyone else for that matter.

Could I possibly make you happy, Gabe? Will you give me the chance?

"I'm not sure I understand."

She needed to back away a little, so she wouldn't scare him off. She sat back in her chair and made sure her knees weren't touching his. Then she tried to explain how she'd resisted getting involved with men because she feared being hurt again. How she'd never been able to make a man happy or keep him, so she'd put all her love into Ben, which smothered him.

"So you've never really dated anyone?" She couldn't read much from his expression, all angles and shadows in the darkness of the porch.

"No. Except for a few dinners out. A few movies and concerts. But all casual. Never anyone I took home to meet my son."

The white of his teeth peeked through his smile.

"Don't smile about this. Can't you see what this means?" The anguish from earlier welled up once again, choking her. She pushed air through her clenched throat. "I failed as a mother and worse than I ever thought. Don't you see? Ben's plummeting grades, his withdrawal, the drinking and experimenting with drugs…all because I pressured him to be the man of the house."

"Oh, Faith." He stood and pulled her up and into his arms.

His soft words and gentle touch were too much. Tears eked out and a sob tore out of her. Not only for the loss with Ben, but also for what could never be with Gabe…and Chelsea. "How can you ever trust me with your child? I make—" another sob shook her "—a mess of everything."

He rubbed her back, then he ran his fingers through her hair. "No, you don't. You're a good mother. And you've been great with Chelsea."

Faith was too drained to speak. She just wanted to slink home and climb back under the blanket.

"I'm sure Ben will come around once he's had some time to process your conversation. He'll realize *he* chose his friends, *he* chose to drink and do drugs. Your loving and protecting your son didn't drive him away."

Oh, how she wanted to believe him. But Ben's perception was so different. "I asked for forgiveness. He wouldn't give it. He's been angry for so long…"

"Then we'll keep praying."

She sat down and wiped her eyes. She couldn't even look at him. "Thank you for praying for us."

"It's my privilege. Plus, praying for you and Ben has helped me start talking to God again. *You've* helped me do that." He sat across from her and tried to lean in to look into her eyes. "Can't you see how good you've been for Chelsea and me?

Had she really been? Was it possible that despite her failings, she'd done some good along the way?

She'd been praying for Gabe, too. To find the perfect woman. Would God answer that prayer, as well?

A squeak sounded just inside the front door, like the creaking of the floor. Chelsea peeked her head out the door. "Oops. I guess I wasn't being too sneaky."

Gabe gave up his chair and Chelsea flopped into it. "So, you two…?"

"No," Faith said at the same time Gabe did.

Chelsea frowned at her dad, then turned back to Faith. "So what's up, then?"

"Nothing. I was just talking about Ben with your dad."

"Oh," she whined. "Is that all?" She slung her leg over the edge of the chair and sulked. "I thought maybe something was going on with the two of you." She threw her arms out in a gesture of surrender. "Are you sure?"

"Chels, why don't you go get ready for bed?"

"You'd be a great match. I say go for it."

"We'll take that into consideration," her dad said as he pulled her out of the chair and pushed her toward the door.

"Man, you got my hopes up, only to dash them. Cold, Dad. Very cold." She laughed as she went inside but didn't look a bit as if her hopes had been dashed. With a quick look at both of them, she said, "Don't rule it out, okay?" She shut the door and sang "God Is So Good" once again.

He sat in the chair Chelsea had vacated. "Sorry about that."

If Chelsea didn't give up on this matchmaker nonsense, she would end up hurt. "Gabe, I think she really has her heart set on us getting together. We have to be careful how we handle our…friendship in front of her."

As if he'd taken the warning seriously, his mouth turned downward. "So you don't think she's just teasing?

"No. I think…well, honestly, she seems to have gotten attached to me."

Concern drew his brows downward, as well. "I see."

"Let's make sure we don't get her hopes up."

"Of course not." He pulled his lips into a tense smile.

It grew quiet. Embarrassment filled the air between them.

Awkwardness—and the hardness of the chair—made her uncomfortable enough that she stood. She rubbed her back. "I should go."

"This wicker is pretty but not practical." He scooted his chair back into place.

"More of Tina's decorating?" She was mortified that she sounded petty and jealous.

"Yes. I wanted a huge, cushy lounger. But she liked the wicker."

More than anything, Faith wanted him to make a move forward. Some sort—any sort!—of move to take over his life and let his late wife go.

Of course, that desire was totally irrational. What was the point?

Still, she couldn't help hoping. "So why not buy that lounger? You'd be more likely to spend an evening enjoying your front porch."

"I'll think on it."

She could tell by the closed expression on his face, by the way he shut down right before her eyes, that he would not seriously consider it.

Heaviness pressed against her shoulders and chest. Ben was still angry and wasn't coming. And now Gabe had once again put up a roadblock.

Keep out, it fairly shouted. *Don't mess with Tina and me.*

And she suspected the man had no idea he was doing it.

That night after Gabe tucked Chelsea in, he took a cup of coffee to his back porch and settled into a chair—which, of course, wasn't comfortable for relaxing. He set his cup down and stomped back inside to grab a pillow off the couch.

Irritated at Faith's suggestion to replace Tina's furniture, even more irritated he couldn't bring himself to do it, he slapped the pillow into the chair and sat on it. Much better. He scooted around, trying to settle. It wasn't comfy, but it was tolerable.

The coffee aroma wafting upward from the mug reminded him of Faith. Poor thing. Her crying had nearly brought him to his knees. He hated to see her hurting.

She was a good mother. He knew that just by watching her with Chelsea. Sure, she may have made some mistakes. He had, too. Was still making them. But Ben had no call to be so hard on his mom. She'd sacrificed a lot for the boy and he needed to quit being so selfish.

Gabe had to show her that people cared about her and thought she was a good person. Surely Ben would come around. But until then, Gabe wanted her to know she was…loved?

The thought sent his heart racing. No, loving her was Ben's job. Gabe's self-appointed job was to show her that he and her church friends *cared.* Yes, he could handle that. He just needed to figure out how.

On Wednesday, Chelsea hung out at the café with Faith for most of the day. The child was ecstatic over something—cheerful, giggling, grinning—all day long. Afraid Chelsea held out false hopes of Faith having a budding relationship with her dad, Faith tried her best to disabuse the notion.

She prayed desperately that God would help her be content with His plan. Her prayer did change a bit, though. She found she still prayed for Gabe to find the right woman for him and for Chelsea. But now she knew she also needed the gumption to move on in her life—for herself and for Ben. So she also prayed that she would find the perfect man for herself.

Though she couldn't envision that new life yet, she knew God loved her and wanted good for her. God would provide.

When Gabe came in the early afternoon to pick up Chelsea, Faith's heart rate doubled.

She wished she could blame it on too much caffeine. But no, it had nothing to do with coffee and everything to do with the gorgeous, kind, wonderful man standing across the counter.

He stopped at the cash register. "Hi."

"Hi." She stared into his beautiful espresso-colored eyes. Yet the intensity of eyes so dark that the pupils were almost indistinguishable from the brown that ringed them left her rattled.

She couldn't move. Couldn't speak.

She had it so bad for this man.

"Um, I'm here to pick up my daughter?"

"Oh! Sorry." She stuck her head in the kitchen. "Chelsea, your dad's here."

When she came back, he leaned closer to her, resting his forearms on the counter. "So how about dinner tonight?"

A silent squeal echoed inside her head. Was he asking her on a date?

"Come join Chelsea and me for hamburgers and hot dogs."

"Oh." Not a date, then. That was good.

He raised his brow, giving her a questioning look.

Apparently, she'd sounded disappointed. "Okay," she said a little too brightly. "That sounds like fun. What time?"

"Six-thirty?"

"Sounds good. What can I bring?"

"Nothing. Just you and your amazing smile."

Disappointment that she couldn't ever hope for a real date made it difficult to smile at the moment, but she managed to anyway.

Chelsea ran out and hugged her dad hello, then they made their way to the door. "Six-thirty," he said as they left the café. His gaze and smile held promise.

Promise of what? Some charred beef and flies on potato salad?

Faith couldn't help the rotten mood that dogged her the rest of the afternoon. She just hoped she didn't scare off her new employees.

She felt sorry for herself as she headed home to rest for a while before changing for the cookout. Even a fun, flirty skirt, new sleeveless top and cute sandals couldn't knock out the frustration that she cared for a man who wouldn't allow himself to care in return.

As she dabbed on lip gloss, she forced away the

disappointment and focused on the positive. A fun evening with Gabe and Chelsea to take her mind off the fact she still hadn't heard a peep from Ben.

She headed out the back door and across the yard. But as she neared Gabe's back porch, she heard voices.

When she rounded the huge crepe myrtle loaded with heavy fuchsia blooms, Chelsea yelled, "There she is."

Faith froze and her hand flew to her chest. A group from the church—Ann, Phil, Olivia, Valerie and others—stopped talking as if waiting on her.

"Surprise!" Chelsea and Valerie called in unison.

Gabe spotted Faith standing at the corner of the porch, staring. She glanced at her watch as if confused.

"You're right on time," he called.

A nervous smile slowly formed. "Wow. A party."

He handed his spatula to Phil and then hurried over to her.

"Did you do this for me?" she whispered.

"Yep. When everyone heard Ben couldn't come, and knew how disappointed you'd be, they wanted to do something special for you."

Her eyes filled with moisture. "Are you kidding?"

"Nope. Come on over. Join the party." The joy of surprising her warmed him inside.

She gave him a quick hug, then released him just as quickly. "I don't know what to say."

"Just tell me hot dog or hamburger. Or both." He put his arm around her and led her to the crowd. As he took his place back at the grill, standing beside the pastor and flipping burgers, he watched as her church family embraced her as one of their own.

Touched by how they seemed to sense her needs, he turned to Phil. "I know she's been here now for what, a year?"

"Yes," Phil said as he placed cooked hot dogs into buns and stuffed them back in the bag to stay warm.

"But it seems like this is the first time she's truly felt at home."

"She's always held herself aloof. But I think it was because of some sort of pain. And maybe you're helping with that?" He eyed Gabe. Then wiggled his brows, teasing.

"We're just friends."

"Uh-huh."

"We are."

"Oh, I'm sure you are. But I detect a bit more these days."

Gabe stared across the grass to where Faith sat in a circle of lawn chairs with Chelsea and Olivia and several others, laughing. "Maybe so. I think I may be ready to move on."

"Tina would want that."

He looked into his pastor's kind, understanding eyes. "Yes, I think you're right. The hard part is letting go, though. Knowing how to do that."

"You'll figure it out in time. There's no hurry."

Phil was probably right. Maybe the first step would be to admit to Faith how he felt. It made perfect sense.

Just one step at a time. Surely he could manage that.

He spun the wedding band on his left finger. When would he be ready to take it off?

Perspiration beaded on his already sweaty forehead. *Faith, you'd laugh if you knew you'd made me nervous.*

He touched his ring once again. It wouldn't be easy to take it off and store it away for Chelsea to have someday. It might even be more difficult than buying that new couch.

Then again, maybe not.

Faith spotted him staring at her. She waved. Smiled.

He smiled back and something inside him changed. It just clicked into place. Like when he discovered a piece of evidence that solved a case.

She spoke to the ladies in the group, then got up and headed his way.

Tina, I think I may be moving on with my life. I hope you approve.

Though she doesn't see it yet, Faith could be a good mom to Chelsea. I know she would love her.

"Hey," she said as she parked herself beside the grill. Her hair shone in the sunlight. Her eyes sparkled like he'd never seen them sparkle before.

"Everyone has been so sweet to try to comfort me over Ben's canceled visit. Thank you for doing this."

"You're part of the church family. They wanted to do it."

"And I've finally been able to open up about why he lives with his dad. And…well, they've accepted me anyway."

"Of course. We're all your friends and we—"

Phil stepped between them, bursting their little bubble of closeness, preventing him from adding that all her friends love her.

Waving his grilling tongs in the air, Phil said, "So, Faith, I kind of feel like I'm taking advantage. But I'm desperate. Hannah can't come on the retreat because she has to work."

She seemed to know where he was going with his request and held up her hand to stop him. "Phil…"

"Ben can't come, and you have your vacation time arranged," he spewed out quickly before she could stop him again. "Come on. Help chaperone the rafting retreat."

A sneaky gleam changed her expression from one of denial to one of…well, sneakiness. "On one condition."

"You name it," Phil said.

Gabe had a feeling he wasn't going to be happy with the condition.

Especially when she hooked her arm through his and laughed. "I'll go if Gabe *and* Chelsea go."

Alarm—or maybe it was more of a thrill—shot through him. He was trapped.

But he realized, with a chuckle, that he was glad. No excuses now. He and Faith would spend the weekend with his daughter and a group of kids.

And the thought made him happy.

Very happy. "Deal."

Their announcement brought a cheer from Chelsea and her friends. They chattered incessantly through the rest of the meal and the roasting of marshmallows and making of s'mores afterward.

As the evening wound down, and everyone had pitched in to help clean up, Velma and Valerie offered to stay with Chelsea so Gabe could drive by the station to check in. Once all the other guests had gone, he walked Faith to her back door.

She stopped before going in, so he leaned against the porch railing, trying to look casual while on the inside he was wound up as tightly as a cocked gun.

"Thank you so much for tonight, Gabe."

"I was glad to do it."

She tried to put her hands in her pockets, but then realized she didn't have any. With a little laugh, she crossed her arms in front of herself. "I learned something tonight."

He wanted to brush her hair back from her face, but he didn't dare go closer for fear she would quit talking. "What's that?"

"That sometimes all you have to do to make

friends is to jump in and be yourself. I shouldn't have waited to be invited."

She had no idea the invitation she was extending with her sweet smile and guileless expression.

"Don't try to play matchmaker for me anymore," he said in answer.

"Excuse me?" She uncrossed her arms and went for her nonexistent ponytail.

It was another invitation. This time for him to close the gap between them.

Gabe smiled as he pulled her into his arms.

Faith wasn't sure what was going on, but she went willingly. She'd wanted this closeness all evening but hadn't dared hope for it. Not with the impossibility of a relationship.

No, she shouldn't want this so much. She pressed her hands against Gabe's chest and leaned her head back to look him in the eye. "What does playing matchmaker have to do with inviting friends into my life?"

"I'm going to follow your lead and try to jump right in."

She sucked in a breath and he had to have heard it.

He smiled as he brushed her hair behind her ear.

Yep. He'd heard all right. And he seemed awfully pleased to have made her gasp.

Her heart ran a sprint even as fear rooted her feet in place. Why did he suddenly seem interested in moving forward? Was it pity? "You're just trying to make me feel better over Ben, aren't you?"

He ran his thumb ever so lightly over her bottom lip and stared at the spot he'd set to sizzling with a mere touch. "I'm just trying to move on with my life." He closed the gap between them. Almost. His breath still teased her aching lips. "I'll be the one who decides who I go out with. Understood?"

The fact that she was within kissing range seemed to indicate he'd decided on her. "You're crazy." The declaration was a barely a whisper. And she wanted to cry, because she didn't have the willpower to back away.

He kissed her then. His lips touched hers gently, molding to a perfect fit. Less demanding than the first kiss. More sure.

She resisted throwing her arms around him. Instead, she reveled in the tenderness of the kiss. But the longing…the ache…

He ended it with a brush of lips on each cheek. Then her nose.

He rested his forehead against hers. "I think it's time I admit I have feelings for you."

She sucked in a breath. Held it. "What?"

A deep laugh rumbled in his chest. He lifted her chin and stared into her eyes. "Please say you'll go out with me. Next week. After the retreat."

She searched his eyes. He was truly serious.

How could he do this when he still loved Tina…

when Faith would surely mess up with Chelsea? "I think maybe you've misunderstood my feelings."

"You can deny it all you want, but your kiss doesn't lie."

Then she had to do a better job hiding the fact she cared. Because it wouldn't take him long to realize this whole thing was a mistake. She wasn't Tina. Could never be such a good mother for Chelsea. Or be the perfect wife for Gabe.

She dragged herself out of the embrace she craved so much. "Sure, there's a strong attraction. But we can't mistake that for true feelings." She opened the door and stepped inside. With her back to him, she clenched her eyes shut. "Thanks again for the great party."

Then without looking at him, she closed the door behind her.

Chapter Fourteen

Gabe was an idiot. He fretted about his actions most of the night. The cicadas outside his window seemed to mock him. By the time he got up in the morning, he realized his error in judgment.

He should have known Faith wasn't at a place where she could consider a relationship. And he'd scared her away.

He needed to be patient.

And do damage control.

"I need your help," Gabe said to Faith at noon when he approached the cash register at the Coffee Time Café. He tried to act as if nothing out of the ordinary had happened the night before.

She scrambled behind the counter and came up with a sleeve of paper coffee cups. Once she ripped it open, she topped off the towering, already full stack. "I'm swamped today. Tell Chelsea I'm sorry."

With a light touch of his hand on her arm, he tried to still her frantic motions. "You know, I was going to plan some sort of party for Chels for a week or so out. But since her birthday is next Wednesday, I'd really like to surprise her with a party on the retreat."

She stopped restocking and finally looked at him. "She'll love that."

Though obviously protecting herself, her eyes held compassion. She had so much to offer if she could get past her fears.

"Can you take an hour for lunch and go shopping with me?"

As if trying to find an excuse not to go, she glanced around the empty café. Then she sighed and settled those kind eyes back on him. "I may have exaggerated my level of busyness just a little. Hang on..." She trudged to the kitchen, and he heard her voice as well as the voice of the new guy.

A couple of minutes later, she emerged apron-free and trying her best to smile.

She cared enough for Chelsea to set aside her objections and to help him. Everything inside him warmed, giving him a sense of rightness.

He helped Faith into the car. They had a quiet drive—yet comfortable. Once they reached the shopping center, he parked and waited, unsure what to do. "Okay, here's where you take over. I'm clueless."

She pointed him toward the department store. "They'll have all the froufrou things I think a thirteen-year-old girl would enjoy."

When she led him straight to the cosmetics counter, he groaned. "Don't even think about it."

"It'll be a gift from me. I want to make an appointment for her to have a consultation to learn how to apply cosmetics the right way."

No wonder she came along. To torment him. "Nope. Won't allow it."

She crossed her arms and glared at him. "You asked me to help. Trust me."

Oh, boy. Those were some mighty big words. Words he wasn't sure he could follow. "You mentioned perfume. I could deal with that."

"I promise I'll come with her and make sure the makeup artist does a totally natural, age-appropriate look."

He squinted his eyes at her. Part of him wanted to let her do this, because it would sure put him in Chelsea's good graces. But he also knew being in her good graces wasn't as important as doing the right thing.

He gestured to all the tubes and compacts and bottles. "Why do all this?"

"Because she's becoming a young woman. And feeling like her dad approves of her femininity is very important to her self-esteem. Esteem that needs to be built, I might add, so she'll be confident around boys and will be smart and strong in her relationships." She glanced down and picked at lint on her blouse. "Strong enough to say no if they pressure her."

It was as if she'd jabbed him with a fist to his diaphragm. "I take it your dad didn't give you that."

She shook her head. "He left us when I was eleven and didn't come around much."

No wonder she had trouble trusting him. Her dad left her, her husband left her…and basically, her son had left her, too. "So from age eleven, it was just you and your mom?"

"Yes. I think my mom cried for a year. She'd cry awhile. Say, 'I can't believe he left us.' Then cry some more."

Which must've made her feel as if it were her fault. "How old were you when you got pregnant with Ben?"

She started to look away, but then faced him straight on. "Seventeen. And so you don't have to do the math, we married quickly and quietly."

Teen pregnancy made a little lip gloss seem harmless. It also made him want to hug Faith and protect her—and to shoot that teenaged Walt. Instead, he rubbed her arm. "All right. You can make her the appointment."

Her smile was reassurance and reward. "She'll be ecstatic."

He watched while she arranged the appointment and bought a gift card to pay for any items Chelsea decided to buy. When she was done, she asked, "What now?"

"Now you've got to help me pick out something

even better than makeup. I can't let your gift be the hit of the party."

She gave him a quick hug and then took him by the hand to lead him through the mysterious world of purses, perfume and jewelry. But he found he was drawn to buying Chelsea a necklace.

"I like this," he said, pointing to a delicate silver necklace with a plain cross pendant. "She loves to talk about God. I think she'll like this outward symbol of her faith."

Faith pressed her arm against his, staring into the glass case alongside him. "Oh, Gabe, it's perfect. It'll mean so much to her that you picked it out."

"You helped."

"Nope. You did this one on your own." She gave him a sad smile. "My dad always sent my mom money and told her to buy me something. And that was only on the years he remembered." She flagged down a salesperson. "Chelsea is a lucky girl."

He wrapped his arm around her shoulders, wishing he could take away past hurts. "And I'm a lucky man."

She disentangled herself as quickly as she could. Once again, he'd pushed too hard. He had to back off.

After he bought the necklace and got it gift wrapped, it was time to leave the store. But they were talking and took a wrong turn. They ended up at the wrong exit, right by the furniture department.

"Oh, look at this," she said as she sank into a cushy,

brown leather sectional. “This would look great in your house. Would hold a gazillion teenagers.”

He stared at it. At her. Then quickly back at the couch. “Yeah, it would look nice. Practical, too.”

He envisioned setting Tina’s sofa and love seat out by the road. But he wouldn’t have to do that. He could give it away to someone who needed it.

A vision of the pieces being hauled off in a pickup truck made his stomach clench.

He ran his thumb over the thick gold wedding band on his left ring finger. Panic seized him by the throat. *What on earth am I doing?* “Come on,” he said in a near rasp. He cleared his throat. “I need to get you back to the café.”

Her face fell. But then she gave him a knowing—sad—smile as she stood. “Okay.”

He took off ahead of her. He needed a little space. Time to deal with his thoughts.

With his hang-ups.

Maybe he wasn’t as ready for this relationship as he thought.

Faith tried to be understanding. Really, she did. But on Friday afternoon as they loaded the church vans and headed to North Carolina for the retreat, she couldn’t help being angry. And relieved. What if she’d fallen for his lines? What if she’d decided to accept that invitation to go out?

It was going to be impossible for Gabe to pursue a relationship with her. With any woman, for that matter. The man couldn't even bring himself to buy a silly couch.

Her insides churned so that she could hardly focus on the girls in her van. Of course, they were absorbed in their own handheld games, texting and chatting.

By the time they arrived at their destination three hours later, she was prepared to avoid Gabe. But then he climbed out of the van he'd been driving, laughing with his group of guys, and he looked up.

When he spotted her, he froze midgrin. Waved. Then he hurriedly spun around to join back in the joking.

No way could she deny the attraction. Or her feelings for him. But even if she thought she was right for him, he couldn't get over his reticence in the furniture-buying department.

In the letting-go-of-his-wife department.

They unloaded and made their way up a steep gravel road to their group of cabins. Dinner was under an arbor at picnic tables. Throughout the meal and the evening program, Chelsea glued herself to Faith's side, almost as if she sensed there was discord between her and Gabe and she wanted to align with Faith.

And she did so even while Parker sat nearby, as if she weren't a bit interested in him anymore.

"Can I have everyone's attention?" Gabe asked once Phil finished with his talk. As the kids quieted, he slipped out of the meeting room, then he came back in with Chelsea's birthday cake.

Delighted squeals ricocheted off the walls. They sang the "Happy Birthday" song.

Chelsea glowed as she made a wish, then blew out the candles. She leaned into Faith. "Don't you wish you could know what my wish was?" She glanced at her dad, then grinned at Faith.

Faith was afraid to guess. But she had a feeling she might be tempted to wish the same thing. So she deflected the conversation with, "Just wait till you see your gifts."

Gabe handed Chelsea the small package and also the envelope from Faith.

As expected, Chelsea burst to her feet in excitement over the gift card and makeover appointment. "Faith, you rock! Thank you!"

Faith stood and gave her a hug. "You're welcome. I look forward to going with you."

Next, she opened her dad's gift. "Oh, Dad. I love it." Tears misted her eyes as she latched the chain around her neck. "I've been wanting a cross necklace. It's perfect."

Chelsea gave Gabe a long hug—longer than was probably considered socially acceptable by teens. But Chelsea wasn't just any teen. And the two of them had been through so much.

"Okay. Let's cut the cake and eat so we can hurry outside for our bonfire," Phil said with tears in his own eyes. "The staff has already lit the fire."

Once they finished the celebration and cleaned up, they headed outside into the dark night with flashlights in hand. Light from the campfire beckoned from across a field.

"Sit by me," Chelsea said as they gathered around a small bonfire for bedtime devotionals.

Thick logs formed seating in a square around the fire pit. Faith took a spot beside Chelsea—who proceeded to hook arms with her. The fire crackled and popped, the flames licking at the cooling night air.

Gabe sat on a log almost directly across from them.

"You should go sit with your dad," she said to Chelsea.

Chelsea gave her a confused look. "I like sitting with you."

She smiled at the girl and patted her hand. What could she do? Still, she worried that Chelsea was getting attached.

As Phil delivered a devotional on having faith through the difficult times of growing up, Faith couldn't help but think of Gabe and Chelsea's terrible time of losing a wife and mother. But God was faithful and they were both healing. And maybe God had used Faith to help just a little. She could live with that, then move on.

Before praying, Phil gave the teens a chance to speak. One of the high school seniors spoke about what God had done in her life to bring her back to the church after straying.

When she finished, Gabe stood. "Phil, I'd like to say something."

Faith's heart began to pound, a slow, thudding *lub dup. Lub dup.*

"I turned away from God when Chelsea's mom was killed in a car wreck."

Kids all around the circle looked at Chelsea, most with sympathy, a few, who apparently didn't know, with shock. Then they all looked back at Gabe.

"But God has been faithful. He never once left me. Even when I was too numb to think about Him. Even when I ignored Him and refused to attend church. Refused to pray."

He looked right at Faith. "But lately, I've found a new desire to talk to God. And I see all the people He's sent to pull me out of that pit."

Her slow *lub dup* picked up pace, leaving her burning inside.

"I owe a lot to our pastor, here. And to other friends from church."

Chelsea squeezed Faith's upper arm. "That would be you," she whispered.

"I hope that no matter what you face as you grow up, you'll know God is watching over you. And that you've got your youth group friends."

The circle remained quiet. Then Phil prayed a beautiful prayer about friendship and the lavish love of Christ.

When he finished, he said, "Okay, kids. Time to get ready for bed." The announcement was met with groans and boos. "Come on, get moving. You have some time in the cabins. Lights out at eleven."

Traveling the hilly gravel road through the heavily wooded campsites, they arrived at the cabins without Faith running into Gabe. Grateful for small favors, she bounded up the stairs to the girls' lodging where chaos reigned. Clothes, hair accessories, toiletries and shoes lay scattered on the ground.

Late to the scene, Faith ended up claiming a top bunk—where they were stacked three beds high. For the next hour, she dealt with pillow fights, homesickness, calls home to check in, showers, a friend spat, more hurt feelings and reconciliation. She climbed to her bunk in the rafters and longed to pass out. But she couldn't still her mind enough to sleep.

Any hope for rest fizzled when she heard a noise outside.

Deciding maybe she should patrol for a little while, she slipped into her clothes and went outside to check around. She walked the path, lit only by the quarter moon and a few well-placed sidewalk lights, from cabin to cabin for about ten minutes. Then when she heard voices inside the boys' cabin, she decided to park herself between the two buildings. Just to make sure no one trespassed.

As she leaned against a wooden fence bordering the sidewalk, the door to the boys' cabin squeaked opened.

She readied to grab some boy by the scruff of the

neck if he dared pass by her in the semidarkness, but the figure that came toward her was no mere teenager. His shoulders were way too broad. His gait too sure.

Gabe came to a stop beside her but didn't look at her. He glanced up at her cabin. "So, are you the girls' sentinel?"

"Self-appointed after hearing noises outside." He hadn't looked at her, but she certainly looked at him—in his shorts and old T-shirt that clung to every muscle.

He settled in against the fence right beside her, his arm brushing hers. "I'll help watch. I just sent three boys back to bed. They had rolls of toilet paper."

"Ooh. Glad you stopped that one."

"They're good kids."

She nodded. "I think what you said tonight really spoke to them."

"I hope so." He finally turned sideways to look at her, his hip and elbow resting on the wooden fence. "I was talking about you, too, you know. You've helped me more than you know."

"I'm glad." She turned to face him but resisted the urge to lean into him, to ask him to hold her. Instead, she rested her elbow near his. "So, are you ready for the big day of rafting tomorrow?"

"Well, I'm glad I let Chels come. She's having a blast. But I can't say I'm ready for tomorrow."

"You'll both do fine."

He raised his free hand as if he was going to touch

her, but at the last second he veered away and shoved it into the pocket of his shorts. He tilted his head to look at the sky. "Beautiful night."

Oh, please, don't talk about the weather. Look at me. Kiss me. Convince me we could do this relationship thing. "Yes. Beautiful."

He sighed. "Look, I'm sorry about yesterday. The thing with the couch."

Sudden tears prickled behind her eyes. "Grieving is a process."

Would the man not move one step closer? She wanted so badly to rest her head against his shoulder, even though she knew staying apart was best.

"Yeah. I guess it'll take longer than I thought."

Cicadas and tree frogs serenaded her. A mosquito buzzed by her ear.

He swatted it away. "I really care about you. And I want this..."

There it was. The big, implied, but. So she supplied it for him. "But..."

"But I may have jumped the gun."

She rested her hand on his chest, the washed cotton of his shirt velvety smooth. She couldn't stand not touching him when she knew how he was hurting. "It's okay. We'll continue being friends. That's for the best, anyway."

He laid his hand over hers and pressed it more firmly against his chest, then wrapped his fingers around hers. He stepped closer. Nuzzled his cheek against hers and inhaled deeply. “You always smell so good.”

She couldn’t do this again. Not this closeness knowing that emotionally he was way far away. “So you like the smell of campfire smoke?” Though she wanted to cry, she managed a little laugh.

He gave her hand a squeeze and stepped away. The response she’d hoped for. The response she’d dreaded. “I’m sorry, Faith. I shouldn’t do this until I’m certain.”

Yeah, he wasn’t certain how he felt about her. Wasn’t certain he could love someone else as much as Tina.

Wasn’t certain he could commit to a woman with her track record. When the one thing Faith needed most was a man who would be fully, and permanently, committed to her.

Saturday morning dawned bright and hot. Perfect for white-water rafting.

The kids were in hyper-gear as excitement and nervousness assaulted them—especially the younger ones who’d never been rafting before.

Gabe couldn’t say he was in any better shape. His blood buzzed with fear for Chelsea as they unloaded from the vans and the guides started grouping them, rushing them to unload their rafts and get to the water because another large group was behind them waiting.

Before he realized what happened, he’d been

grouped with five middle-school boys…and Chelsea was nowhere to be seen.

"Here, hold this." He jammed his paddle into one of the boy's hands and hurried off in search of his daughter.

He found her at the front of the group, with four other girls and Faith, as they were setting their boat into the water.

"Oh, it's ice-cold," she squalled as she stepped into the shallow loading area.

"Chelsea, come on and get in my boat."

"Is this your dad?" asked their guide.

Chelsea rolled her eyes. "Yes. He's way overprotective."

"Come on, man. She'll be fine with me. Let her go with her friends." The early-twenties guy, tanned and buff, reeked of cockiness.

"I'll watch her," Faith said. "I'll put her right beside me."

"Get in, girls," the guide called. "Dude, you need to get on back to your raft." He nodded up the hill.

Gabe glanced back. His boys were struggling to lift the huge raft and drag it toward the water. Should he jerk Chels out of the water and make her ride with him?

"All right, three strokes forward," the guide called to the girls, moving them slowly away from him. "Not like that. Slow, even strokes—all together. One…two…three…"

Faith waved him toward his boat. "She'll be fine. I promise."

How could she promise that? Hadn't he promised that he'd always take care of his wife?

"Hey, Mr. Reynolds, we need your help," one of the guys called.

Okay, God. Watch over her for me.

He rejoined the boys, who seemed relieved to have his help. And probably relieved to have him there just for reassurance. They seemed more nervous than the girls had. Of course, when their guide told them to paddle, and they managed only to go in a circle, the boys were worried about the coolness factor.

He vowed to try to set aside *his* worries and give them a good trip down the river. So each time the guide called out an order, he counted out loud to help them paddle simultaneously, the act of vocalizing a distraction from the worst-case scenarios raging through his mind. "One…two…three…four…" *God…keep…Chels…safe…*

The mantra played out for the next two and a half hours. At some point along the way, he'd begun to relax. They'd survived a couple of rapids, and he'd been able to spot Chelsea's boat up ahead a few times—enough to reassure him that she was okay.

Their guide pointed ahead. "All right, guys. This is it. The final rapid's coming up. The biggie. We need to keep to the right unless you want to get flipped."

Most of the boys tensed up. But Parker, who'd

been the lone brave soul in their raft because he'd been down the river earlier that summer, yelled, "I want to ride the bull."

Their guide grinned. "Okay. Climb up there and get ready. And hold on tight."

Gabe couldn't believe it when Parker climbed over the seats and sat right up on top of the very front of the raft. He wrapped one hand in the rope just like a bull rider. Then he threw the other one up to mimic the bull-riding motion.

The rapids came into view.

And Gabe watched the boats ahead of them go one by one into the swirling mass of angry water.

"Okay, guys. Remember, stay to the right. Don't do what that other boat is doing. They seem to be having some trouble." He stood from his post at the back of the raft and shielded his eyes. "That group of girls…oh, man. It's going to be rough."

Just as Gabe's boat hit rough water, his stomach sank. He searched the rafts in front of them, looking for Chelsea's head. Looking for Faith's head. But the helmets made it hard to tell who was who.

"Four strokes forward on the left. Hard!"

"One…two…three…four…" *God…keep…Chels…safe…*

"Okay, hold up. Wait…" The guide jammed his own paddle into the water. "Now, four backward."

"One…two…three…four…" Gabe yelled over the roaring of the water. *God…keep…Chels…safe…*

Their boat moved round the right side of mounded

rocks and barreled easily through the raging rapids. The guide and boys cheered.

As they moved out of the worst of the rushing water and started into smoother territory, angling for the take-out point, he spotted the girls' boat that had gone to the left of the rocks. It sat folded nearly in half—almost like a taco shell—as the guide pushed against a rock with his paddle and yelled something at the girls.

The raft eased just a little, then suddenly, the current grabbed it and yanked it from its spot. One side of the boat dipped down, and as it did so, he recognized Chelsea's hot-pink shorts. And then all of a sudden, the dipped side yanked even deeper and Chelsea tumbled into the water.

"Chelsea!" His heart slammed into his chest as he started to jump in the water.

The guide grabbed him and held him in place. "Wait. She'll be fine if she just rides it out."

Her head bobbed, but she put herself into the position they'd been taught to assume if they fell out. She appeared to be bumped around some, and would probably be bruised. But as long as her head remained above water, Gabe could breathe. As soon as the water slowed, she waved over at his boat.

His knees nearly buckled in relief. Poor thing had probably been more worried about scaring him than about her own safety.

Gabe knew Faith would be relieved, as well.

He looked back at their raft as it made its way through the rapids toward Chelsea.

And Faith wasn't in it.

His heart hit his toes. *Oh, dear God, no. Please, not again.*

The girls' guide struggled to push their raft off another rock. He acted panicked.

"What's going on?" Gabe asked his guide.

"Can't really tell. Looks like they've got two or three out of the boat."

"Let's get over there and help."

"No way can we go back. But Zeke is the best. He'll get 'em out."

Gabe's breathing grew ragged and short as he searched for a sign of Faith. *God, help her.*

Still, no helmet appeared.

Chelsea remained in the water near the take-out point. She was knee-deep and searching.

Lord, You can't let anything happen to Faith. Chels would never recover. He sucked in air and shuddered. *Oh, God, help me. I love Faith. You can't take her away, too.*

Suddenly, Chelsea threw her arms in the air and cheered.

The girls' guide reached his paddle over the far side of the raft and then grabbed someone by the life vest and pulled her in.

Was it Faith?

Please, Lord, let it be Faith.

A body slid into the boat and didn't move. It took

every bit of his willpower not to jump into the water. But he knew any attempt to move upstream would be futile.

He scanned the girls remaining in the boat. They laughed and smiled. Surely, Faith hadn't drowned. She must just be lying there recovering.

A heartbeat later, Faith's laugh carried across the water. As the raft moved closer, he could distinguish her voice. She finally pulled herself up onto a seat. Then she looked at him and gave a weak smile.

Fury overtook his fear. His muscles tensed as his fists clenched. *No way.* No way would he get involved. No way would he let himself love her. Not when she did things like fall overboard in a raging river.

He jumped out of the raft and pulled it to the shore. Once all his boys were safely on land, he grabbed Chelsea's hand and tugged her along with him toward the old, beat-up school bus that would take them back to their vans.

"Hold up, Dad. Let's wait for Faith."

"No. Get on the bus."

"But Dad…"

"I said get on the bus." Something red caught his eye. Chelsea's knee. "You're bleeding."

Faith was so weak, she could hardly climb out of the raft when they landed near shore. Her muscles quivered. Her voice quivered as well as she gave her girls instructions and herded them to the bus.

Gabe and Chelsea were off to the side with one of the guides examining and bandaging Chelsea's knee.

She needed to check on the girl, but the last thing she wanted to do was face Gabe.

Sick dread clutched her as she approached. Because she knew he would never again trust her with his daughter.

"Hey, are you okay?" she asked Chelsea, avoiding eye contact with Gabe.

"I'm fine. But how are you?"

"Just weak." And shaken and bruised.

Chelsea reached one arm around her waist and squeezed. "You scared the life out of me when I couldn't find you anywhere. Did you get held under?"

She could feel the tension radiating from Gabe's body at her side.

"I'm fine. The river let me up after a few seconds."

"Let you up?" Gabe asked in the most menacing voice she'd ever heard from the man.

She finally braved looking him in the eye. His dark eyes drilled into her. He was furious.

"I don't really know what held me under. I think maybe my foot was stuck. Or maybe it was just the water." And she'd thought she'd never breathe air again. "But then I popped up like someone had shoved me to the surface." She smiled at Chelsea, not wanting to frighten her. "It looks like Chelsea, here, got the worst of it."

"No biggie," Chelsea said.

Gabe glared at his daughter as if to say that, yes, it really was a biggie. "I'll drive her to the emergency room as soon as we get back to camp. They say she needs a few stitches."

"Chelsea, I'm so sorry. I thought I had you. But the raft bucked so hard…"

"It's not your fault. I panicked and didn't keep my foot wedged where I was supposed to."

Gabe took Chelsea's elbow and pointed her to the bus. "Come on. We're holding them up."

His reaction clearly said he thought it was Faith's fault. It was because of Faith that Chelsea was even on the trip. Because of Faith's weak grip that she'd bounded out of the raft. No doubt Tina would not have let her daughter fall out. In fact, Tina probably wouldn't have allowed Chelsea to go on the trip in the first place.

"I really am sorry, Gabe," she said to his back as she climbed the steps behind him.

He didn't say a word. He followed Chelsea until they found an available seat, then he scooted in beside his daughter and stared at the floor. Or maybe he was staring at his daughter's temporarily bandaged knee—a reminder of how she couldn't be trusted to take care of his child.

Chapter Fifteen

Sunday evening after the vans rolled into the church parking lot, tired kids with sunburned noses emerged as relieved parents waited for a hug.

Gabe told each youth goodbye, then he mechanically loaded his and Chelsea's bags into the back of his car. The youth group wouldn't be meeting that night, so Chelsea hugged her friends goodbye. They were teary and bummed as if they wouldn't see each other again for ages.

In reality, it would probably be less than a week. But they were having trouble coming off the spiritual high of a retreat.

Sometimes it was hard to go back and face the real world.

And didn't he know it.

Back in the real world, he had a job waiting. Had a lonely, quiet house waiting. Had empty days waiting.

Of course, he should be thankful he had Chelsea to fill his life. She was the one good thing.

And Faith?

He located her across the parking lot where she tirelessly hugged each girl goodbye. But he could tell she was stiff and sore by the way she bent so gingerly. Being tossed out of the raft had been hard on her.

Much to his aggravation, he wanted to go comfort her. To tell her it was okay. That he wasn't mad about Chelsea—that it wasn't Faith's fault.

He wished he could tell her he was actually angry because somewhere along the way, she'd stolen his heart. And he just couldn't allow it. Couldn't risk playing that game again.

So instead, he quietly rounded up Chelsea and vowed not to let Faith get under his skin.

But as he watched her walk to her car, he couldn't bear that she thought she hadn't protected Chelsea to the best of her ability. He knew where her mind would go. She would blame herself.

"Chels, I'll be right back."

He walked over to Faith's car and pecked on the window.

She rolled it down.

"I want to make sure you know I don't blame you for Chelsea falling out of the raft."

"I'm so, so sorry. I tried to hold on to her."

"I know. I was just angry in the heat of moment. I was scared." *That I'd lost you.*

"Thanks." She started her car with a guarded smile.

Everything had changed. He could see it in her

eyes. Between their discussion about his inability to move on and his lashing out over Chelsea, he'd driven a wedge between them.

"See ya around." He forced himself to walk away, so he wouldn't say things that shouldn't be said.

He climbed in the car with Chelsea and drove toward home, hoping his failure wouldn't hurt her, as well.

Chelsea made a squawking *bwok, bwok* noise. "Chicken."

"Pardon me?" He glanced over, and she sat with her arms crossed, glaring at him.

"You're a big fat chicken."

"I have no idea what you're talking about."

"You love Faith and now you're scared."

He looked at his more-perceptive-than-ever-imagined daughter through squinted eyes. "Tell me what I'm scared of, oh wise one."

"Of Faith dying like Mom died."

Adrenaline surged through his body, making his foot hit the gas pedal too hard. He eased off. If Chelsea saw, then who else could see it, as well? "I think it's best if you let us deal with this."

After a moment of silence while staring out her window, she said, "You better let me keep hanging out at the café."

How could he do that? Every day he'd have to go by there and have contact with Faith. "We'll see."

"Please don't mess up everything that's good right now."

Her plea socked him in his already tender gut. But he couldn't make any promises. "I don't know what'll happen, Chels."

They arrived at the house and carried their stuff inside. It smelled stale. But as they walked in silence to their respective bedrooms, Chelsea's disgust radiating off her in waves, he thought he could smell Faith's perfume.

Faith, I wish I could tell you the truth. But I can't let anything come of it.

He could almost imagine Faith shaming him. Of course, what he really heard was Chelsea's taunts. *Chicken.*

Yes, he was a chicken. But he'd rather be a lonely chicken instead of a grieving man who had to watch his daughter go through the ultimate heartbreak again.

Yes, he was a chicken. Not so much scared of loving. But scared of losing love yet again.

So he had to back away from Faith.

As awful as it seemed at the moment, he knew it would be better in the long run.

On Monday morning, Faith decided to continue working even though she was still technically on vacation. She had nothing at all to do at home. Nothing except agonize over Gabe and the tension she felt between them.

He'd suddenly lost all interest. Between Faith trying to push a new sectional sofa on him and then letting his daughter nearly drown, he'd apparently decided a relationship wasn't an option.

And even though she knew it was for the best, losing that bit of ridiculous hope left her…in a funk.

As the blue mood started to descend, she forced herself to look beyond her own pain and focus outward. Just like Ann would do. Which reminded her to check on her friend.

Faith ran by the hospital to see Ann, who'd had shoulder surgery that morning. After a groggy Ann lectured her to be patient with Gabe, Faith went back to the café to catch up on paperwork.

The afternoon rolled around quickly. And still no word from Chelsea. Or Gabe. Not that she expected to hear from him. But she'd thought surely Chelsea would come by to hang out for a while. And she found she missed having her there.

A little chirping sound from her cell phone distracted her from the worry. It was a voice mail from Ben. *Having fun. Games went well.* Short and to the point.

Though it was a perfunctory message that Walt had probably forced him to make, it was nice to hear from him. Still, there was no indication of forgiveness.

She tried returning Ben's call, but got no answer. Before closing her phone, she decided to compose a text message to Gabe. *Missed seeing Chelsea today.*

She inserted a smiley face, but then backspaced

and deleted all she'd written. So she tried again… *Can we talk about what happened this weekend?*

Her finger hovered over the send button. But she backspaced and tried one more time. Only this time, nothing would come.

With a huff, she facetiously typed *Why don't you just get with the program and ask me out?*

That felt good. Who knew typing could be cheap therapy? So she sent her thumbs flying across the keypad to add to the message. *And while you're at it, quit hem-hawing around and go buy a stupid couch. Just get over it already. It's been five years. And I LOVE YOU. Doesn't that count for something?*

Thinking and typing the words sent a shock wave through her body. But it was time to admit the obvious.

Yes, she loved him. She had for a while. And it drove her crazy that she couldn't do anything about it. But, oh, it felt so good to vent to her cell phone, to let her feelings out. She closed her eyes.

Lord, help me know what to do with these feelings.

She clutched the phone to her. *Oh, God, it hurts so much to know he doesn't trust me with Chelsea. I can never be a part of their family. And even if I were the perfect mother, he doesn't love me enough to take the steps he needs to heal.*

"Faith, are you okay?" Juanita asked.

She jerked her eyes open and batted away tears. "I'm fine. Just praying."

"Chelsea's on the phone. Or I can ask her to call back later..."

"No, I'll get it in a second."

As Juanita headed out to the dining room, Faith went to hit the backspace button on her cell phone to delete her rant at Gabe. But the text message wasn't there.

After her stomach hit the floor, her pulse began to throb in her gut, then throughout her body. *No!*

She took a deep breath to stave off the panic. No way had she sent the message. She'd probably just brought up another screen. Or had deleted it while praying.

Chelsea was waiting on the café line. She couldn't search her cell phone now.

She laid the phone carefully on her desk so she wouldn't accidentally send the awful message. Then she hurried to pick up the landline.

"Faith!" Chelsea sounded distressed even though she spoke softly. "You've got to do something. Dad asked Hannah out."

Every fiber of Faith's being froze, stealing her very breath. *This is too much.* "Are you sure?"

"I heard him on the phone arranging to pick her up for lunch tomorrow."

Faith held herself together, making sure not to say anything upsetting to Chelsea. *So this is it, then. He's moved on to Hannah, the more appropriate choice.*

Even though she'd expected it, her chest ached...

throbbed. "Well, we've been praying about this for a while."

"But he loves *you*. I know he does. You *have* to do something."

Faith tried to block out the desperation in Chelsea's voice as well as the desperation trying to drag her into a heap on the floor. She pushed the pain inside to deal with later. Privately. "Chelsea, honey, sometimes things don't work out the way we want them to. Sometimes God has other plans—even better ones."

Chelsea sniffed. "Can't you tell him how you feel?"

The thing was, Gabe surely knew. But his feelings weren't strong enough for him to make the leap. "God will work out everything. We need to keep praying."

Faith's words didn't offer much comfort, but before Chelsea hung up, she promised to trust God.

Feeling fragile, as if she could fly apart at the touch of a feather, Faith carefully picked up her cell phone. She had to find that text message to Gabe. What if it got sent *now,* after Gabe had moved on to Hannah?

She clicked on the messaging symbol. There was no text message on the screen. It had disappeared.

With trembling fingers, she checked the only other place she knew of, the folder that showed all messages that had been sent.

No recent messages sent to Gabe.

She collapsed against the back of her chair. But her relief was short-lived. What if by some strange happening, it got sent but didn't register?

Outrageous scenarios bombarded her. What could she do?

Lord, please, please let the message just be lost somewhere in cyberspace. Please don't let him read it. I can't imagine losing his friendship.

Pain welled up to nearly unbearable. Friends. It's all she would ever be with Gabe.

Juanita cleared her throat from the doorway of Faith's office. "You're a popular woman today. There's a handsome man out here wanting to see you."

Dread chilled her blood. "Thank you," she said through teeth that didn't want to open.

She couldn't avoid the confrontation. She just hoped Gabe would forgive her for the awful message.

She stood on lead-weighted legs and forced one foot in front of the other. When she reached the dining room, she took a second to peek over the top of the espresso machine. She discovered not the top of Gabe's dark hair, but a familiar blond.

"Ben?"

He gave a sheepish wave. "Hey, Mom."

How many times had she imagined this moment? Ben showing up to surprise her. Ben smiling to see her. Ben *coming home.*

Her heart swelled in her chest. Love for him

was almost overwhelming. She hurried to him and grabbed him into a big hug. "But you're in Florida."

"Do I look like I'm in Florida?" He laughed as he pulled away, the awkwardness making him blush. "My message was to throw you off. I decided to leave as soon as the games ended so I could surprise you." He shuffled his feet, kicking at something invisible on the floor. "I missed you. And I've been thinking a lot and wanted to tell you it's okay. You know, the stuff we talked about."

He'd skipped Disney World for her? She didn't say a word. Just held her breath as she stared into his precious blue eyes and let him take his time.

"I do forgive you, and I'm sorry for being so hard on you."

Tears prickled behind her eyes. They were words she'd longed to hear. Words she'd dared not dream of. She took hold of his hands. "Thank you for forgiving me, sweetie. I'm glad you came."

"Good." He huffed in relief. "I've felt awful for saying that stuff."

"It needed to be said."

"Yeah, but I realized I've made the last few years difficult for you. Especially before I moved to live with Dad. I guess I've also felt guilty for leaving—didn't want to come visit you and be reminded." He looked into her eyes as if asking for something. Maybe forgiveness?

"Those were rough times and we both made bad

decisions. Me, my stubbornness. You, the alcohol and drugs. But don't ever feel guilty for moving to your dad's. It was the best decision for you at the time."

Her six-foot-one son hugged her. "I'm so glad to be here. But I only have two days before I have to go home to get ready for the next trip."

"That's okay. We'll enjoy every minute." She flagged down Juanita and Randy and made introductions.

"Go on home. We've got it covered," Juanita said.

"I plan to do that. I'll take that vacation, after all." She grinned at her son and led him back to her office.

The cell phone sat on her desk mocking her. "Oh, Ben, you have to help me with this contraption."

"I'm no expert on cell phones."

"You're young." A simple statement that said it all when in reference to dealing with technology. "I was typing up a text message that I, uh, decided not to send." Her face burned. As much as she'd like for him to find the stupid message, she hated to think of him reading it. "But it's disappeared. Can you find it for me so we can delete it?"

He started scrolling through the menu. "It's probably in your draft folder." With the punch of a few buttons, he located that folder. "To Gabe?"

"Yes." She reached for the phone.

He snatched his hand back and laughed. "Let's see what's so urgent..."

Panic seized the air in her chest. “Ben, stop. Give it here.”

She tried to reach for the phone, but he stood nearly a foot taller, and she didn’t have a chance when he held it aloft. “Let’s see…”

He stared at his outstretched hand, reading. She could tell that he actually read some of the message, because he grew still and his grin dropped into a frown.

He held the phone out to her. “I’m sorry. I was just kidding around. Didn’t know you were serious.”

She sighed. “It’s okay. You had no idea I could be so ridiculous, did you?” She deleted the message.

“So what’s going on?”

“It’s a long story.”

“Well, I have two whole days.”

She nearly cried. All the years of thinking Ben would never come back to her. Of worrying that they’d never be close again… And now finally, her son was here. She patted his back, then rubbed up and down, amazed at how muscle-bound and strong he’d grown. “Okay. I’ll fill you in.”

She hooked her arm through his. “Come on. I need to show you off around town before we go home. And I’m afraid I know one man, Daniel, who’ll want an autograph.”

Joy blossomed inside, so full and penetrating that it nearly hurt.

In the late afternoon, Gabe had a lull in work, so he dropped by the house to relieve the sitter and pick up Chelsea for a visit to check on Ann, who'd just been released from the hospital. When they arrived at Ann's house, a truck sat out front that had Fulton County tags. There was also another car with a metro county plate that he thought belonged to her grandson.

"I don't know, Chels. It looks like she's already got company. Maybe more family."

"You know she won't mind. I need to talk to her."

"About what?"

She turned sideways in her seat and rolled her eyes. "About you and your goober-headed move to ask Hannah out. Miss Ann needs to pray harder."

"I didn't ask Hannah out."

"I heard you do it. On the phone."

He resisted fussing at her for eavesdropping. He also resisted sighing. Instead, he calmly said, "It's for a lunch meeting to discuss the Sunday night youth program."

Her mouth fell open on a gasp. "No lie?"

"No lie."

The grin that spread from her chin to hairline could have powered Corinthia for a week. "Then there's still a chance for you and Faith."

"Your matchmaking services are no longer needed. Why don't you just ask Ann to cancel the prayer request?"

"Can't do it. We need God to fix this mess you made."

Oh, the faith of a little child. "I didn't make a

mess. I simply made a decision about what's best for you and me." *A decision to protect us from loss.*

"Well, God's just going to have to change your mind."

A chill raced along his arms, raising the hairs, even while he opened the car door to a blast of heat. What if Chelsea was in the right? What if God really was working in his life to find him a mate?

Of course, he still had to figure out how to deal with the fact that he loved Faith.

As they reached Ann's front porch, the door swung open.

"Oh!" Faith clutched her chest.

A tall young man stood behind her. When he grinned, Gabe could see the resemblance. The boy scanned Gabe from head to toe, noting the weapon. "You must be Chief Reynolds."

"And you must be Ben." He held out his hand. Could this be good news for Faith?

Ben reached around his mom to shake. "And that means you're Chelsea."

"That's me." She shook Ben's hand, also.

Faith's obvious joy put a lump in Gabe's throat. Yes, it was good news. And it was about time. She deserved this happiness.

"Ben's here for a couple of days," Faith said. "We were just heading home."

Gabe cleared his throat past the sudden surge of emotion. "Well, good to see you." He nodded, then ushered Chelsea inside.

"Wait." Ben planted himself in the doorway. "Chief Reynolds, Chelsea, we'd love to have you drop by tonight. Maybe for dessert?"

Faith's eyes widened. They hadn't discussed this ahead of time. But she was quick to recover. "Sure, we'd love to have you."

He knew he should say no, should try to stay away from her and keep Chelsea from getting any more attached. Loving another woman was too risky.

"We'll be there," Chelsea piped in. "I'll bake cookies just like Faith showed me." She cut a glance at Gabe and then she seemed to mouth some kind of silent message to Faith.

Faith looked as confused as he felt.

Chelsea kept nodding her head as if trying to get some point across. "Everything's okay," she said slowly, eyes wide and with an exaggerated smile. "See you after dinner."

He shook his head as his daughter rushed inside, calling for Ann.

He turned his attention back to Faith and Ben. "I guess we'll see y'all tonight."

Gabe would be hard-pressed to call the evening anything but perfect. Awkward at first, yes, but with Chelsea and Ben hitting it off so well, they'd all relaxed into a comfortable night on the back porch—as if it were something they'd done forever.

Chelsea and Ben picked at each other like a couple of siblings. His daughter's eyes beamed from the attention of a *big brother.* She laughed more than she usually did even with Valerie.

"Hey, got any more of those cookies?" Ben asked.

"Yep. Inside." Chelsea hopped up to go get them.

Ben jumped up. "No, I'll get 'em."

She followed him through the back door, asking, "You think they're as good as your mom's?"

"Better," he whispered.

Faith smiled from her relaxed position on the lounge chair next to his. "I'm so blissfully happy right at this moment that I don't care what anyone thinks of my cookies."

He rolled to his side and stared at her. "I'm happy for you and Ben. Truly happy."

She angled to face him. "I guess my job now is to move on with my life and live it to its fullest. No pressure on him. I'll just be there when he needs me. And he's promised to call more often."

He couldn't help but wonder if she was trying to send him the same message. *Move on with your life.* Of course he knew in his head that he needed to. He just hadn't yet found a way to take that step to push past the fear.

But then nights like tonight made him wonder. He could almost imagine…

This feeling of contentment. Of completeness.

The sense of everything being all right.

Faith bumped his chair with her foot. "What are you thinking about?"

A life with you. His heart thudded slowly but strongly in his chest, so slowly that it seemed to slow time.

In what felt like half speed, he sat up in his chair and faced her. Then he gave her hand a tug to pull her into the same position so they were sitting knee to knee.

Could he do this? It seemed the perfect idea. Everyone would be happy, especially Ben and Chels.

Especially me.

Yet he couldn't tell if the blood pulsing through his body in slow motion was anticipation or fear. Either way, his heart was about to burst out of his chest.

"Gabe, did you hear me?"

He could barely hear himself think over the rushing sound in his ears. Definitely some fear. But how could he pass up something so perfect? "Um, yes. I, uh—"

She looked concerned. "What's wrong?"

He looked into her eyes and knew there was no way he could ignore the feelings between them. No way he could ignore the sizzling attraction, either. "I think we'd be good together. All of us."

"What?"

He hated to see the confusion on her face. Knew he probably wasn't making sense.

God, I'm trying here. Are You giving me a tiny

nudge? Because what I need is a big shove off this cliff. "I'm saying—"

The door burst open. Chelsea barreled out with a refilled plate of cookies. She spotted Faith and him sitting close with hands held. "Oh!"

When she slammed on the brakes, Ben ran into her back. He pointed off in the distance. "Hey, Chels, what's out in those woods behind the house?"

"Woods? Oh, back there?" She slung the plate of cookies onto the table, rattling the glass. "Oh, um…a creek. Come on, I'll show you."

Ben gave them the biggest grin ever as Chelsea took his hand and tugged him off the back porch, saying, "Race you."

They were gone in a flash, just a glimmer of light clothing hurrying through the moonlit yard.

When he turned to face Faith once again, he sensed her tension. Or maybe it was the viselike grip on his hand that gave him the first clue. He gently squeezed her hand. Then he helped her stand. He pulled her close—something he'd been dying to do for days.

Only he couldn't relax into it. He was too scared. Scared to tell her how he felt. Scared not to tell her. Scared she'd reject him. Scared she'd accept him.

When they were together, Faith seemed happy. Chelsea was happy. And now even Ben seemed happy. Surely Gabe could make the leap to happy as well—if only he could risk trying.

"Gabe?"

"I'm saying I've been an idiot. Running from my feelings. Afraid."

She plunked back into her chair as if her legs had given out. "What?"

He once again sat knee to knee with her. But he didn't take her hand this time. She didn't look exactly thrilled with him at the moment. "I know this seems crazy—that my actions have been all over the place. But when I couldn't find you on the river—" He didn't even want to think about that fear again. "You scared me to death. Because you've become so important to me."

Her mouth remained turned downward. Her eyes…so sad. "Oh, Gabe."

"No, don't look unhappy. This is good. I can't ignore the truth. That you're good for us."

She stood and walked to the edge of the porch. Stared off into the distance.

He stood behind her and put his hands on her shoulders. "I've finally found the woman who makes my daughter happy. Who makes *me* happy. And with all four of us together tonight…well, I want this for all of us."

He felt like he was rambling. She wasn't jumping in as he'd hoped.

He turned her to face him. His heart resumed the slow-motion thudding. "Faith, will you marry me so we can be a family?"

* * *

Faith couldn't have heard him right. "Marry you?"

"Yes."

Even though he looked as if the words were choking him, for one flash of a moment her heart soared as she considered it. But that was just wishful thinking—and ignoring the facts. Like having Gabe and Chelsea depending on her for happiness? Was she crazy? She'd messed up years with Ben and was just getting back on track.

Plus, she'd be a fool to allow herself to be plopped into Tina's position like that. Which was all Gabe was doing. Sure, he cared. And it broke her heart that he was trying so hard to move on and provide for Chelsea. But if there was one thing she knew, it was that she needed someone who would love her fully and be totally committed to her. Otherwise, she'd always be afraid he'd leave her like Walt had left her.

She reached out and ran a finger over one of his shirt buttons. It would be so easy to accept, to settle for less than total devotion. And when he covered her hand with his, she nearly accepted.

"Gabe, I love you. In fact I've been crazy about you for a while. But I need someone who's crazy about me, too. Not someone who's looking for a mom for his daughter—even as much as I'd like to be that mom."

"No, I'm not just looking for a mom for Chelsea. I do love you."

The look on his face said otherwise. He had the look of someone with a noose around his neck.

Not the look of a man proposing to the love of his life.

Tears burned behind her nose. She blinked as quickly as she could. "You can't suddenly change so much. You haven't been ready for the commitment I need. And I'm just not sure you'll ever be ready."

He started to say something, then stopped.

"As badly as I want to accept, I can't do that to myself. I'm sorry."

He pulled away. Straightened his shoulders. Back into tough cop mode. "Yeah. Me, too." He massaged the back of his neck but made brief eye contact. "Thanks for dessert. Just send Chels on home when they get back."

He strode off her back porch and headed home.

The man of her dreams said he loved her. But he didn't love her quite enough.

Chapter Sixteen

Even as Gabe's shock and disappointment began to wear off, the next week dragged by like an eternal stakeout. And watching Chelsea mope didn't help one bit. She had quit asking to go to see Faith at the coffee shop. She'd quit asking to hang out with friends. She'd even given up on liking Parker—because "romance isn't worth the pain and suffering."

And where has she gotten that idea, Gabe?

Disgusted with himself, he sat down with a nearby Bible. It was the one Chelsea had been reading.

When he flipped it open, he found Tina's name in the front. He zipped through the pages, hoping God would lead him to something that would speak to him. Would lead him to something he needed to read.

He flashed past some yellow highlighting, so he backed up a few pages until he found the passage.

The first part of the verse gave him a jolt. *There is no fear in love; but perfect love casteth out fear…*

Fear had certainly made him hold out on Faith.

Perfect love. God's love.

Could it cast out his fear?

He'd been stingy with his love, even while Faith had been so generous.

But he'd told her he loved her.

Thinking back to that night, though, made him cringe. If he was totally honest, hadn't he felt just a little bit of relief when Faith had turned him down? If he'd felt it, then she'd probably seen it.

Oh, Lord, I've hurt her. Help me know what to do. Help me love the way You want me to.

Faith had been right about him. He hadn't been ready for a commitment. He wasn't sure he ever would be.

And she deserved better.

As Faith pulled into Ann's driveway, her cell phone rang.

The call gave her the first bit of hope she'd felt in days. But she shoved that silly hope back into submission. It was probably one of her employees.

"How's it going with Gabe?" Ben asked without so much as a hello.

"The same."

"Then you're both crazy. He loves you. Just give him time to figure it out."

She wanted to cry for the hundredth time that

week. Though everything was good with Ben, she found her day-to-day existence lonely. Disappointing. "I love *you*. And I miss you."

He sighed, then laughed. "I love you, too. See you in two weeks."

Just give Gabe time to figure it out? As if he was going to wake up one morning and decide he was ready to commit to a lifetime with her?

What planet did Ben think she lived on?

After gathering the cleaning supplies from the back of her vehicle, she knocked on Ann's door and then went on inside. Ann stood at the old farmhouse sink trying to wash dishes with one hand while the other arm rested in a sling.

"Are you supposed to be doing that?"

"Yes. I'm fine. Almost like new." She glanced at Faith. "You look awful."

Faith rolled her eyes. Which made her think of Chelsea. And almost made her cry. "Gee, thanks."

"So even though God has this all worked out, you and Gabe are still being stubborn?"

"I told you, he's scared of commitment."

"He's not the only one who's scared."

"I beg your pardon?" She tried to relieve Ann of the dish cloth, but Ann wouldn't turn it over.

"You're just as blinded by fear as he is."

A little tingle shot through her. Surprise. But maybe a tad of recognition of the truth? "But Ann—"

Ann stopped her with the wave of a dripping

finger. "I want you to remember—there are no perfect situations. Don't waste time trying to attain something that's not possible this side of heaven. You and Gabe put God first, and you'll have a good, solid foundation."

Her, fearful? Waiting for perfection? As she carried over a skillet from the stove, it occurred to her that she *had* been scared Gabe couldn't commit long term—that he might leave her when things got tough. She'd also been afraid she wouldn't be able to fill Tina's shoes. Tina's *perfect* shoes.

Surely, those were legitimate fears. "But he hadn't shown me any indicators that he could move on and commit to me. Then all of a sudden he was ready to join our families?"

"Oh, pooh. He's one of the committing-est men I know. But he's just as scared as you are. And here you are setting unrealistic expectations. Give the man—and yourself—a break."

Ann slipped the skillet into the sink. "Now leave me to finish these. And if you have to do something, I'll let you clean my bathtub. I'm not up for that yet."

"Gladly." She reached for her bucket of supplies and left the kitchen. Maybe some scrubbing would take her mind off Gabe.

She squirted cleanser in the bathtub and attacked it with a sponge. The repetitive motion made her shoulders ache, but it was a good ache. And when she finished, the sparkling-clean tub made her smile.

Too bad all the polishing and scrubbing couldn't fix her life. Because no matter how hard she'd always tried to keep everything in her world perfect—and everyone happy—it hadn't worked.

Maybe Ann was right.

She'd been aiming for the impossible when only God was perfect. And He loved her just as she was.

I don't have to be perfect to be loved. The thought resonated deep inside, giving her hope.

Maybe she had been too hard on Gabe. Surely he could mean it when he said he loved her—even while still holding on to the past just a little.

Surely she could deal with a silly couch that his late wife had picked out.

As she moved on to the vacuuming, she decided she wanted to do something nice for him, something that would show she thought Tina was worth honoring. Worth remembering.

It was the least she could do for the woman who had birthed Chelsea.

Chelsea...Gabe. She missed them so much.

Chapter Seventeen

"I'm so proud of you. You're growing up," Chelsea said to Gabe as if she were the parent.

"Ha-ha." Yet, Gabe had to truly laugh at his daughter's teasing. "I guess this is a big step for me."

"It's about time, that's all I can say." Chelsea leaned against him and put her head on his shoulder. "Thank you."

They sat side by side on the front porch steps. She had her overnight bag beside her and her pillow in her lap. He'd made the big move. He'd agreed to allow her to go to her first sleepover at Valerie's house. He was trusting God to take care of her. "Behave, okay?"

"Always."

Faith would be so proud of him, too. He just wished he could tell her the news. Could share with her how difficult it had been to turn over his daughter to God, yet how happy he was at the same time.

Faith, I wish I could just pick up the phone and—

He sucked in his breath. He'd just thought of Faith. Not Tina.

And when he looked back, he realized he'd been doing it the last couple of weeks.

"Oh, man."

Chelsea's head popped up off his shoulder. "What?"

"I've been thinking of Faith."

"Well, duh." She laughed. "I should hope so, since you're in love with her."

Chelsea made it sound so simple. He loved Faith. He should quit being an idiot and do something about it.

Generous love. Like you ask of me, Lord. Even if it has no guarantees.

Lord, I'm ready to move ahead. Help me find the strength.

Olivia and Valerie pulled into the driveway with a loud honk of the horn.

"Valerie's as excited as I am." Chelsea laughed as she stood up and pumped her fist in the air in a victory dance. "Slumber party today. Cell phone tomorrow."

"Dream on."

She laughed as she ran down the steps. "See ya, Dad."

"Whoa." He caught up to her to kiss her goodbye. "Hey, Chels, do you mind if I do some redecorating while you're gone?"

"Cool! I'd love it."

He waved at them as they drove off, then hurried to his car. He had a couch to buy. And a phone call to make.

Faith couldn't have been more surprised by a phone call. But Gabe calling to ask her to babysit was probably just a fluke. He was probably in a jam and had no other options.

She tried not to let her hopes climb. She would just go over there and give him the gift—the shadow box she'd purchased to display mementos of Tina. Then maybe they could at least be friends again.

She grabbed the bag and marched herself to his back door.

When he opened it, he smiled, and her world melted right back into his as if they hadn't spent any time apart. She grinned back. "Hi."

"Thanks for coming." He stepped away from the door and motioned her inside.

Before she lost her nerve, she held out the bag. "For you and Chelsea."

His brows arched in surprise. "What for?"

"Just open it."

He pulled it out of the bag. "Um… What is it?"

She wanted to laugh, but bottled-up nervousness made it come out as more of a squeak. "It's a box to hold mementos. I thought maybe you could put some of Tina's things in there. Things that'll be special for Chelsea to keep…things you'd like to keep."

He stared at the box. His throat bobbed up and

down. "Thanks," he said in a raspy voice. "It'll be a perfect place for my wedding band."

Her gaze zipped to his left hand. No ring. Then it zipped back to his face. *Oh, my.*

That look he was giving her…

Like the look he'd given her way back when he'd kissed her.

Her stomach fluttered and floated.

"Come here. I have something to show you." He held out his hand for her.

"Where's Chelsea?"

"She was my excuse to get you over here." He raised his chin and puffed out his chest. "She's actually spending the night at Valerie's."

Faith's mouth flew open. "You didn't."

His proud smile turned to a full grin. "I did. And I couldn't wait to tell you."

She put her hand to her chest. Thought she might burst with pride. "You did good."

"With your help. And God's." He held out his hand once again.

This time she took it and followed him to the living room. When she stepped into the room, she gasped.

The old couch and love seat were gone.

She gripped his hand tighter as she finally exhaled.

He politely ignored her gasp and walked her around to the new leather sectional, the one they'd seen at the department store. He let go of her hand and sat down.

Then, with the sweetest smiled on his face, he patted beside him. “Join me.”

Tears flooded her eyes. She knew the invitation to join him was much more than a mere invitation to sit beside him. But was it willingly? “Gabe, I’m sorry if I’ve pressured you to do this. I tend to pressure the people I love.”

“And I tend to hold back from the people I love.” He patted once again. “I did this because I wanted to. Because I realized I’ve been thinking only of you the last few weeks. Today when I was so proud of myself for letting Chelsea go, I didn’t think of Tina. All I could think about was calling you. Telling you about this huge step.” He patted a third time. And he looked scared that she would refuse.

He didn’t need to ask her again. She practically dived beside him as she threw her arms around his neck—strangling him in her usual manner. She tried not to cry, because she wanted to be able to see him. She blinked and pulled back far enough to look into his dear face. “Thank you for this.”

He took her hands and swallowed. “Faith, I love that you’re kind and generous. I love that you’re a good mother to Ben…and to Chelsea. I love that you put God first in your life. And I love how you make me feel when I’m with you.”

As he knelt in front of her, her heart thudded so strongly she could hear it in her ears.

Gabe looked into her eyes and smiled. "Quick disclaimer. I didn't have time to buy both a couch and a ring today, so I chose the couch."

Biting back a grin, she leaned closer and said, "I love a man who has his priorities straight."

He grinned at her. "Good. Because now I know what I truly want. I want to spend the rest of my life with you." His took her hand in his. "Faith, will you marry me?"

He was calm, confident. This time, there was no trace of doubt. She saw sureness in his eyes. Sureness and love.

Joy soared through her making the tears overflow. "Yes. Yes!"

He joined her on the new couch—*their* couch—and he kissed her. More than thorough, he tilted her face for a better fit. His lips moved over hers as if to make up for lost time.

It only made her crave more.

He pulled away and pressed his forehead to hers. "How soon can we plan the ceremony?"

She ran her hands over his strong shoulders and stared at his lips. "Oh, I think long engagements are way overrated."

A deep chuckle rumbled in his chest. "Yeah. Way overrated, especially when I'm ready for us to start our life together." He kissed her again. Then he brushed his cheek against her hair. "I love you, Faith."

Sweet music to her ears. "I love you, too."

Epilogue

Gabe paced back and forth, up and down the hallway, past old family photos and ending at the newly added shot of Faith, Ben, Chelsea and him after a baseball game. He smiled at the four of them and then proceeded to pound on the bathroom door. "Come on, Chels. You'll make me late for my own wedding."

"I'm hurrying."

"Well, I'm counting to ten, then I'm leaving."

"Daaad."

"Did you just roll your eyes at me?"

"Yes, sir. Sorry." She huffed. "Can you come help me?"

Scary girl things lay behind that door. He stared at it for a full five seconds. But Faith would shoot him if he showed up late, so he turned the knob and walked inside.

Compacts and tubes littered the counter. A color diagram of a face lay propped in front of the mirror.

It looked as if someone had been finger painting with sidewalk chalk. "What's that?"

"Faith drew a picture to remind me where to put the different colors of eye shadow and the blush."

Love—for Faith and for his daughter—melted away the stress of the day. He leaned against the counter and took hold of Chelsea's chin to tilt her face toward him. "Hmmm." He glanced at the diagram. "Looks perfect to me. Nice job."

"Not too much?"

He stared into eyes the color of Tina's. But Chelsea had kept her hair short and looked more like him every day. The female version anyway. "Nope, not too much. You're thirteen years old, after all." He winked at her. "Now, let's hurry to the church before Faith changes her mind."

"Oh, Dad. You know she'd never change her mind. She's head over heels for you."

"And she's head over heels for you, too." He kissed his daughter's forehead. "Your mom would be so proud of the young lady you're growing up to be."

She wrapped her arms around his waist and clung to him. "I love you. And I'm so glad to see you happy again. Mom would approve."

He pressed his face against her hair and breathed in the fragrance of this child of theirs and knew he was the most blessed man alive. "Yep. She would."

Faith sat in the tiny bridal room at the back of the church staring into the mirror, trying to touch up her makeup. But her hands wouldn't stop shaking. Rather than risk a big rosy slash of lipstick across her cheek, she set the tube down and frowned.

About the time she decided she needed to go find Ann for help, Chelsea burst into the room. "We're here!" The girl came to a dead stop just inside the door. "You look amazing."

"Thanks. Except look at these pale lips. I can't seem to hold my hands still enough to put on lipstick."

Chelsea came to her side and grabbed the tube. "Nervous, huh?"

"I'm surprised. I was fine till five minutes ago."

"Here, I'm an old pro now. Let me help." She giggled as she rolled up the berry-colored lipstick and made a few quick strokes across Faith's bottom lip. When she tried to do the top lip, she contorted her own mouth in all sorts of directions.

Faith laughed while trying to hold still.

"Hey, it's hard to color inside the lines on someone else."

When Chelsea finished, Faith studied herself in the mirror. She found a couple of feathers of extra color that she'd fix once Chelsea left the room. Didn't want to hurt her feelings.

She smiled at her future stepdaughter. "Thank you, sweetie. You look so pretty. You did a wonderful job on your own makeup."

"Thanks to your instructions."

Faith stood and took hold of Chelsea's hands. "I'm

so glad the four of us will be a family now. God has truly blessed me."

"Me, too." She hugged Faith. "Don't forget. On the honeymoon, you have to talk Dad into getting me a cell phone."

Faith laughed and ushered her out the door to meet up with Gabe.

With one last check in the mirror, she smoothed her hand over the beaded bodice of the long, flowing ivory gown of her dreams. The dress she'd never had as a teenaged bride. When Gabe had heard that story, he'd insisted she have the wedding she'd always wanted.

And now here she was, marrying the man God had picked for her, the man who would love her fully and forever.

She picked up the bouquet of blush pink roses, inhaled the rich fragrance, then quietly walked to the back of the sanctuary where Ben waited.

He looked so grown in his tuxedo as he proudly held out his arm for her. "You look beautiful, Mom. And so happy."

"The happiest day of my life."

He kissed her cheek. "You deserve it."

When the first chords of the bridal march sounded, she moved down the aisle on the arm of her son. Sun shone through the brightly colored stained glass illuminating her church family, there to celebrate their union and to show their love and support.

Gabe and Chelsea stood side by side at the altar with matching smiles.

As she came closer, all her focus zoomed in on Gabe. So big and strong and handsome in his black tux, standing there waiting. For her. Faith Hagin. Soon to be Faith Reynolds.

Their gazes locked and held as her son handed her over to Gabe, and he turned to stand beside her. Ready to promise his love to her. *Till death do us part.*

* * * * *

Dear Reader,

Thank you for once again taking a journey with me to small-town Georgia. I hope you've enjoyed spending time in a new fictional town with new characters I've grown to love.

A Family for Faith was inspired while I was flying home from a writers' conference. Across the aisle, and up one row, a dad sat by himself with a young daughter. He was trying to fix the bow in her hair and was not having any luck at all. I just ached for him and his daughter, wondering if there was a mom in the picture. But I was also touched at how gentle and persistent he was, and that he tried so very hard with that silly bow. Right then and there, I knew I had to write a story about a single dad with a daughter who was hitting an age where she really needed a mother figure.

So this book is dedicated to that loving father who was trying so hard. And to all of you out there who are raising or helping to raise children. May God bless you and multiply your efforts.

Thank you so much for reading my book! I love hearing from readers. Please tell me what you think about *A Family for Faith*. You can visit my website, www.missytippens.com, or email me at missytippens@aol.com. If you don't have internet access, you can write to me c/o Steeple Hill Books, 233 Broadway, Suite 1001, New York, NY 10279.

Missy Tippens

QUESTIONS FOR DISCUSSION

1. Have you ever found yourself holding back love out of fear? How did you overcome that fear?

2. In this story, Faith Hagin feels like she failed as a mother. Have you dealt with guilt or feelings of inadequacy in any area of your life?

3. In the story, Gabe Reynolds needed to control things in his life. Do you find you have the same tendency? Do you think it might be something you could turn over to God?

4. Is there someone in your life who has suffered the death of a spouse? How might you help them in their grief?

5. What do you think is the theme, or premise, of this story?

6. One of the theme verses (listed in the front of the book) is First Corinthians 13:13. What does this verse mean to you?

7. The other theme verse is First John 4:18. What does this verse mean to you?

8. How do you see these two verses relating to the story?

9. Faith worried about planning the perfect vacation with her son, about competing with Gabe's late wife (whom she saw as perfect), and about finding someone who would love her totally (and maybe perfectly?). Do you or someone you love tend toward perfectionism? How does that affect you or others around you?

10. Chelsea was a pretty typical twelve-year-old. Did you find you could relate to her? Could you understand her wish for her dad to find a girlfriend?

11. Have you ever been white-water rafting? Or have you ever done something that pushed you beyond what you would normally be comfortable with? Can you share about the experience?

12. If you have pushed yourself beyond your comfort zone before, what did you learn from it? What did you learn about yourself?

13. Were you ever involved in a church youth group? Was it a positive experience?

14. If you're involved in a church, has your church family been a support to you in any way you'd like to share? If you're not involved in a church, is there somewhere nearby you'd consider visiting?

15. Do you know someone who's loving and supportive like Miss Ann was in the story? How can you stretch yourself in learning to be more generous with love?